THE **SEEDS** OF
WINTER

THE SEEDS OF WINTER

ARTILECT WAR BOOK ONE

A.W. CROSS

GLORY BOX PRESS

The Seeds of Winter

Published by Glory Box Press
British Columbia, Canada.
gloryboxpress@gmail.com

First edition, 2017

ISBN 978-0-9950991-7-3

Cover design by germancreative
Interior design and formatting by Glory Box Press
Editing by Danielle Fine

FOR H.

PROLOGUE

In 2005, Professor Hugo de Garis predicted that by the late 21st century, the ability to create artilects—hyper-intelligent, sentient machines—would splinter humanity.

Three distinct factions would form: the Cosmists, those attempting to create artilects; the Terrans, those opposed to their creation; and Cyborgists, those who advocated the melding of human and machine.

This division would ignite a war causing billions of deaths and the end of the modern world.

In 2040, his prediction came true.

"Will they be autonomous? Yes. Will they have free will? Yes. But they will also be connected to each other. It is essential to our survival and to theirs. Cyborg brains are not the same as human ones, much as we prefer to believe otherwise. Their connection must be made carefully, gradually, insidiously. Planted in such a way that the still-human parts of their minds will accept it without question. That way, the connection will be established before they're even aware it's happening."

—Mil Cothi, Recommendation #13; Pantheon Modern Program Omega-117.

01

AILITH

I'd been having the dream for as long as I could remember.

It was always the same. I ran across a field as vast as an emerald sea. Heat rose from the grass where my feet fell, rippling up my bare legs. My body was small and thin, my tiny hand clutching a string which led up, up, anchoring a kite. The kite itself was strange: a man but not a man, smooth and shiny, with only the suggestion of a face. Silver ribbons streamed from his golden arms and legs like shooting stars as he chased behind me, straight and true.

In the middle of this green ocean rose a single tree. I raced toward it, my body expanding, stretching. When I reached the tree, he was waiting, as always. I could never see his face, only his mouth, naturally mournful, curving into a smile as he offered me a lover's hand. When I took it, my own was grown-up, strong. He gazed upward to where the kite had become tangled in the branches of the tree. When his eyes returned to me, he was no longer smiling, his mouth once again downcast. And as always, I dropped his hand and began to climb.

Halfway up, I skinned my leg on the rough bark of the tree. Blood welled up and out of the wound, but it wasn't my blood; this blood was much older, its original host long dead. It snaked down my calf as the tips of my fingers brushed the edge of the kite. Straining, I caught its body and crushed it in my hand.

A gust of wind blew through the leaves, wrapping pale amber tendrils of hair around my face as I climbed back down the scarred trunk. It was easy because I was lighter now—all the blood from my body had soaked into the soil and been devoured by the roots. When I reached the ground, he was gone, and I was nothing but paper and bone. I pressed my face into the now-moist earth so that the wind couldn't take me. I was the seed.

We have triggered the waking sequence. As of yet, six subjects are unaccounted for, including O-117-9791. Whereabouts unknown. It would seem the secrecy that kept us hidden for so long is coming back to bite us in the ass. We'll give them a few days to get their bearings, then initiate the homing signal. We never should've separated them; we thought spreading them out would increase their chances of survival in case we were discovered. We were wrong. Hopefully, they'll fare better than the five still alive here at the compound. Losing them all at this point is unthinkable.

—*Mil Cothi, personal journal: May 27, 2045*

02

AILITH

The hard ground beneath me softened, yielding to the heaviness of my head. I sank into it as far as I could, grateful for the comfort.

Maybe I'm dead. Maybe it was all too much, and I died. That would make sense. But can you think when you're dead? That is what I'm doing, isn't it? Thinking?

Open your eyes. My body refused to obey.

The air was crisp and fresh, not the thick, sweet air of the hospital, and although the surface beneath me was definitely a mattress and not blood-soaked earth, it was not the familiar stiff vinyl and threadbare sheet of an in-patient cot. No, the blanket draped over me slipped too softly through my fingers to be ward-issue.

4

Take a deep breath.

A rhythmic pressure was building in my ears. With every beat, an aching strangeness bloomed inside me.

Is that my heart? Why is it so far away?

Open your eyes.

A scream split the cool air, a searing pulse inside my skull.

Not my voice.

A familiar sharpness lanced through me, hot and dazzling. My fear had always felt like that: a jagged brightness that began in the bottom of my spine and fanned out like the thorns on a rose.

Open your eyes.

Finally, my eyelids opened. Not the hospital. I was in a bedroom, if the furniture was anything to go by. I hadn't seen furniture like that for a long time—not since I used to visit my grandmother—all ornate swirls and leaves carved into the stained wood. Thick curtains covered the window, blocking any hint of natural light. What thin light there was came from a single bulb, but even in the dimness, the room seemed…dusty. I reached out with one finger and scraped a line down the side of the nightstand.

"I've never been that good at cleaning," a voice said.

He was a titan, filling the entire doorway. Or was the doorway small? I couldn't decide. I was having trouble concentrating. He stepped forward, closer to the light. Young, but the dark tattoos on his face made him seem older.

I don't remember him. I don't remember how I got here.

I can't sit up.

My bones seemed to creak as I strained against the thick leather binding my chest, my elbows unable to find purchase in the soft bedding. Something tore, but I couldn't tell if it was the restraints or me. Vomit surged in my throat. I was going to suffocate.

Rapid footsteps sounded to my right, punctuated by heavy breaths. My body arched; my spine twisted.

I will break.

A hand like a block of marble dropped down onto the center of my ribcage, crushing me against the bed. A face hovered over me; a forehead pressed into mine. His deep brown irises were laced with gold and framed by long lashes; they reflected my own gray ones back at me as he stared without blinking.

Why am I not terrified?

"Hold on." Golden eyes narrowed, and the fabric ripped as he freed my ankles. One solid kick was all I managed before my stomach at last betrayed me. Apologizing under his breath, he tore off the remaining restraints and rolled me roughly onto my side. A few more seconds of heaving, and I dropped my head into the cradle of my arm.

"Ailith."

A cold, damp cloth covered my forehead; another wiped at my mouth.

The screaming started again, and my back arched against my will.

"Ailith." The sound was soft and soothing. Familiar, somehow. The pressure in my ears receded, and my mind began to focus. When the next scream stabbed my brain, I kept still.

"Help them." I tried to keep my voice even. The scream had dissolved into sobs. "Please."

"Help who? Ailith, we're the only ones here."

That couldn't be true. If it was, who was crying?

The restraints. I'd forgotten the restraints. *He's dangerous. He's done something to me.*

My heel skidded in my vomit as I scrambled off the bed

6

and away from him. As I backed into the corner, I searched for something to use as a weapon. I wouldn't be able to overpower him, but if I made him bleed enough, I should be able to escape.

I've never seen this room before.

But it didn't feel like his room either. Unless he had a thing for elaborate floral oil paintings and trainspotting, nothing in this frozen, uninhabited room belonged to this man.

His hands were raised before him in supplication. "Ailith."

"Stop saying my name! Who are you?" My voice came out high and thin, and that pissed me off. I snarled at him, hoping I appeared demented enough for him to stay away, that my wobbling legs seemed more like the weaving of a venomous snake.

"My name is Tor. Do you remember anything?"

I stopped scrabbling, trying to focus and remember. Time did not seem to be working properly. The answer was in my mind, but it fluttered away before I could grasp it.

He took a step forward.

"No!" My hand closed around something solid and heavy, and I threw it with all my strength. It struck him hard in the mouth, and I prepared to run. In my mind's eye, I leaped over him, stomping on his neck for good measure.

He remained standing; my missile fell to the floor.

I'd tried to kill him with an antique perfume bottle—a sharply-cut crystal perfume bottle, but still—and now I was going to die in a haze of bergamot and clary sage.

His lip had split where the bottle hit him. Blood smeared down his chin. He didn't seem angry; if anything, he seemed amused, his eyebrows arched and his mouth curled up on one side. That should've alarmed me, but I found it strangely comforting.

"I expect," he said, glancing down, "that was quite expensive."

I peered over the bed on my tiptoes. However badly cut his lip was, the bottle had gotten it worse. It lay in sad little shards at his feet.

I rose onto the balls of my feet again, not sure whether to attack or try to escape past him. A thrumming started in the space behind my eyes, and the rose in my spine began to bloom.

"Ailith." My name, again.

"What are you?" I whispered.

It was his turn to be confused. Tilting his head to the side, he regarded me as if for the first time. "Ailith, I'm a cyborg. Like you."

Of all the answers I'd expected, that was the last. I didn't have time to think about it, though, as the thrumming reached a fever pitch, cool air filled my mouth, and I was blind.

In the darkness, a cable appeared. It led from me, thread-like, into shadow. Another emerged. Then another. Thousands of them, all bound to me. Some shone through the darkness, blazing with light; others were barely visible, their beam extinguished. The first thread drew me in, pulling me down its length before I could understand.

A door appeared. There was a number on it. 479.

"What makes this generation of cyborg unique is the combination of the organic and inorganic at the cellular level. That is to say, every single cell will be cyberized and watched over and replenished by the nanites. They will look completely human, be completely human, but without many of the physiological limitations we now experience. And once we've perfected that, we'll be able to lift the limitations on their minds. Their potential will be limitless."

—Mil Cothi, on the development of Pantheon Modern Program Omega-117.

03
NOVA

The number on the door was 479. Made from cheap black plastic, each numeral was bolted into place too tightly, bowing inward around the screw. I took my keycard from my pocket and slid it down the lock. This door was the same as every other door leading into every other house on the street. Even the street itself was the same as hundreds of others, part of an orderly network. I never knocked. What was the point? Nobody would come to the door to let me in.

The reek as I entered the hallway was typical: stale and heavy, with an undercurrent of human waste. I went straight to the window and slid it open. Although the air wafting in wasn't exactly fresh, it cut through the thicker smells. An improvement, no matter how small, though I only pleased myself. The other two people here didn't care, didn't bother to open their eyes to see who was standing in their living room.

I checked the time. Only 2:45 in the afternoon. Early yet. The doctor wouldn't be here for at least another fifteen minutes, but I was impatient; I wanted to get it done. I continued to stand at the window, gazing over the rooftops capping the endless rows of uniform housing units surrounding the city center. The center itself was studded with high-rise buildings holding offices, gorgeous apartments, special entertainments. Vancouver. I envied the people who worked and lived there. I bet they didn't have to breathe the stench of shit all day.

2:50. I turned toward the center of the room. Two women reclined, facing the window. Sisters. They were unclothed, a soft blanket covering each from chin to toes. Built in the lower half of each chair was a receptacle. The smell emitted from here, albeit fainter now that the window was open. I emptied these containers every few days, sliding them out and replacing them without disturbing the occupants.

Although their heads were shaved, the women still had the oily odor of rarely-washed scalp. Their eyes were closed, the smooth surface of their lids rippling periodically. The sister on the right giggled and chatted; the one on the left smiled coyly, uttering only a few gentle whispers. My nose wrinkled. Their laughter and expressions were awkward, as though they had forgotten how. I rubbed my thumbnail with my index finger, making quick circles.

2:58. The front door opened; Lars had arrived. We nodded to each other.

"Nurse." He knew damn well I wasn't a nurse, no more than he was a doctor. He worked for the government, same as me. Another woman stood behind him; she was to play midwife, pulling an outsized case containing the incubator behind her.

We were processing the woman on the left today, removing the baby fully grown from the embryo we'd implanted thirty-eight weeks ago. Mei. Her name was Mei. I tied up my hair and went to work.

Removing the feeding tube from Mei's nose revealed a darkened line on her face, thrown into stark relief by her pallid, sun-starved complexion. I lifted her blanket, exposing her naked body to the air. She didn't react—they never did. Her skin was moist and doughy,

10

with the odor of overcooked pasta. I started to retch and rubbed my thumb again, quickly, where Lars couldn't see. He'd think I was losing my nerve.

She let out a small sigh, but it was nothing to do with us; the parts of her nervous system that perceived pain were disconnected. I adjusted the chair so she was lying on her back, and reached between her legs to shave her. The sight of her withered thighs, the saggy skin with its mound of overgrown pubic hair, made me want to pinch her softness, to punish her for this vulnerability. Instead, I swabbed disinfectant over the freshly shaved parts and up over the lower half of her swollen belly.

The midwife checked her vitals then signaled to Lars. He made the incision over a previous one, low on her abdomen, curving down, around, and up again. Yellow fat bulged from the cut. He worked quickly, slicing through the layers until he exposed her uterus. Several more cuts, a tug, and the midwife cooed as she rushed to wash, dry, and powder the baby so quickly it didn't have time to cry. The midwife seemed pleased, her face flushed and bright.

Lars finished closing Mei up, sealing the layers with a surgical adhesive. While he washed his hands and changed his clothes, I cleaned her and inserted a new feeding tube. By the time I finished, Lars and the midwife were ready to leave.

Lars shook my hand. "Last day today, isn't it? We'll be sorry to see you go."

I bet you will be. Not too many people around with my moral flexibility. Out loud I said, "Yes. I'm sorry to be leaving. But, when you get the call…"

I saw them to the door then returned to Mei, shaking out her blanket and draping it lightly over her again. Her eyelids twitched back and forth, reacting to a world I couldn't see. I stroked her face gently, torn between scorn and pity. When the cybernetic Completely Immersive Virtual Reality Systems first came out, no one had expected them to produce such a real experience.

It had been too real. Users stopped responding to any other

11

stimulus, including their own basic needs. Millions died with virtual swords and guns in hand while the real-life battle for their lives was fought and lost in their hospital rooms. Those who survived were incapable of readjusting to the real world, even with rehabilitation. But they made effective donors for those who didn't want biomechatronic parts, so these 'houses' kept them in trust, allowing their continued survival in both worlds for our needs in this one. My parents, if they were still alive, were in one of these houses. I sometimes wondered if they'd been kept together.

My finger was on my thumbnail again, circling, circling. I needed to go outside, to get away from here. I'd thought I would savor my final day in this job simply because each time I did something it would be the last. The last day to wipe the drool off someone's chin, to bandage their stumps, to look the other way. Yes, I should've been glad, but I couldn't wait for it to be over.

What a shame I had nowhere to go to celebrate. Just my apartment, with its threadbare carpet and peeling wallpaper. After tomorrow, I wouldn't have to live there. Oh, no, not with the deal I'd made. I would be special. True, it came with a price, but everything did. And I was used to carrying out orders that others might deem…unsavory. That was why they'd chosen me.

They told me I was going to change the course of the world, that I had an extraordinary purpose. I would be the savior of the human race. I wouldn't end up like my wards, forgotten, degraded. No, I would be remembered forever.

Tomorrow, I would enter the program at Pantheon Modern. Tomorrow, I would become a cyborg.

"It sounds like a bad joke, doesn't it? A cyborg, an android, and an artilect walk into a bar. What's the difference between them, you ask? A cyborg is a human being whose physiology has been enhanced by machines, to perform like a machine. An android, or robot, is a humanoid machine, but dumbed down to perform the functions of a human. And the artilect? Well, that's just short for artificial intellect. Androids could arguably be considered artilects. But the ones everyone's getting all worked up about, the real artilects, would appear human but possess an intelligence far greater than our own and have the potential for sentience. And therein lies the problem."

—Emily Fraser-Herondale, Of Gods and Monsters: The Rise of Artificial Intelligence

04
AILITH

"Ailith? Ailith?"

His hands were heavy on my shoulders. I was sitting on the bed, the edge sagging under my weight. The duvet was turned inside out; it was one of the few things in the room not covered with dust. The man—Tor?—knelt before me. "Are you okay?"

"What happened?" My finger circled the bed of my thumbnail. I could still feel my anticipation of what was to come.

Except, it wasn't *my* anticipation. I'd never worked with CIVR addicts, never even seen one. But it hadn't felt like a

13

dream either; everything had felt real, had *smelled* real. It was like I'd been in someone else's mind, watching from behind their eyes. I'd known her thoughts, felt what she'd felt, but I'd had no agency of my own.

Only one thing was clear: she'd been about to become a cyborg, like me. Like *us*.

"You seemed to black out for a moment."

"I was… I don't know. It was like a dream. I was in a house. There were…" I suddenly remembered that I was a captive and flung myself backward. Or at least, my imagination did. My body stayed firmly rooted on the bed, held immobile by his iron grip.

"Let go of me!" To my surprise, he did. And actually had the nerve to look offended. *What the hell is going on?* "What am I doing here? Why was I tied down?"

"What do you remember?"

Nothing. "I— *Tell me!*" For just a moment, my words were outlined in a jagged radiance.

His eyes widened, and his shoulders snapped back.

"Where are we? Why did you tie me down?"

"We're in the Kootenays. You…you were having seizures. It was like you were trying to wake up but couldn't. I didn't want you to hurt yourself. It's only been for the last week."

I searched his face for deception. *He's telling the truth. I think.* I relaxed. *The Kootenays. Shit.* The Kootenays was a mountain region far from home.

His shoulders slumped as though released, and he took a small, gasping breath.

It was time to stop planning my escape; I was completely at his mercy for the time being. But it was more than that. I may not have known this room, but he felt familiar, safe. I was sure of it. If he had meant me harm, why would he have bothered to make sure the duvet was

14

clean?

Clean duvet? Tied you to a bed? Yeah, seems legit to me, the more sensible side of me snarked.

I ignored it.

"Why am I—are we—here?"

"Can't you remember anything?"

"I was ill. I was in the hospital. I was going to have an operation." I remembered the ward linen, scratchy against my broken skin. My green-eyed nurse; her android assistant. But was that *this* time? Or was that months ago?

"I was having an operation," I repeated.

He nodded encouragingly. "Do you remember why?"

"I was dying."

"What else?"

He was right. There had been something else. My stomach. For the first time in years, the skin was almost smooth.

"Ailith?"

I had forgotten to answer him, distracted by the lack of ridges and puckers.

"Pantheon Modern. I was in the Pantheon Modern program." My voice sounded far away. I remembered it all. My illness. The application for the Pantheon Modern Cyborg Program Omega. My acceptance. Haste. And then, pain. "It was too soon."

"Yes. But you survived. And here you are." He smiled, pleased that I remembered.

"Here I am." I echoed, "Why am I *here*?"

His smile faltered. He grabbed a chair from the corner of the room and set it in front of me. He wouldn't look at me, but the ashen color of his skin told me that something bad had happened. *The war.* When I'd gone into the hospital the final time, rumors were swirling that the conflict between the Cosmists and the Terrans was at

15

breaking point. The Pantheon Modern Program was rushing, trying to establish itself as a mediator between the two.

"The war?" I asked. "Has it started?"

He ran his fingers roughly through his hair. Too roughly.

"Tor?" His name was easy on my tongue. Intimate.

He leaned toward me and peered into my eyes. "Ailith, the war is over."

"Over? Surely that's got to be a world record for the shortest war in history. I only went into the hospital a week ago." But even as I said it aloud, it sounded hollow. I was too thin. My scars were practically gone, and I was in a dilapidated house with a strange man. A man who was like me.

"How long?" I whispered.

In his strong hands mine were dwarfed, small and fragile. His eyes never left my face. "Five years."

No air was left in my lungs. I didn't understand.

It's true, a voice whispered in my head.

But it couldn't be true. Losing a day or two of my memory was one thing, but *five years*? Never. Which meant only one thing: he was one of *them*, and he'd abducted me from the hospital.

My coordinator for the Cyborg Program Omega had warned me about them. Extremists who disagreed with the advanced cyberization the Pantheon Modern program had proposed, even though it was supposed to have been a secret. It was the only time Terrans and Cosmists had worked together to destroy a common enemy: me and others like me. Only once we were out of the way could the war over the artilects truly begin.

If this Tor was one of them, I was in trouble. But it didn't make sense. Yet, if it wasn't that, then what he was

16

saying *must* be true, and I'd slept for five years while the rest of the world decided my fate.

The room was starting to lose clarity again, the buzzing in my head building to a crescendo. Whatever was going on, I needed to leave. I had to get somewhere safe; then I'd find out what was really happening.

His eyes were still on me. The mattress springs groaned a quiet protest as I slid off and began to sidle toward the door. *This is madness.* I had no chance of getting away from him. But he didn't move. Only his gaze followed me as I crossed the bedroom and slipped through the doorway.

The front door was across the next room. Like the bedroom, this room had a fine coating of silvery dust on every surface. The footprints going forward and back across the hardwood floor were the same; he wasn't lying when he'd said we were alone. An elaborate fireplace cradled the remains of a fire, the smoldering red embers the only living color in the room.

The same thick curtains as in the bedroom were drawn over these windows; I couldn't tell if it was day or night. Not that it mattered, because I was going regardless. He still hadn't moved, and I didn't know whether to be frightened or bold.

Fuck it. I'm going with bold.

I tried to walk calmly to the door but about twenty feet away, I lost my nerve and sprinted. In my imagination, his hands were only a hair away from the back of my shirt. The floor would hurt my back when I hit it; he would stand over me in victory and chuckle at my foolishness.

But he didn't move. When my hand closed around the cold knob, I wasted a precious second looking back at him. His head was down and his hands were on his knees, as though he was bracing himself against a storm. I took a deep breath and opened the door just as one of the threads

17

tethered to my mind flashed. And I was blind. Again.

R,

Just wanted to let you know we've received confirmation of A-98C334's acceptance into the MPCPO-117. Told you it would work. We're lucky that the parents were still alive —no way could we have gotten enough genetic material from her alone. I kept expecting we'd get busted any second, but they didn't seem to suspect a thing.

I'm sorry I argued with you about how much we should tell her — I was worried she'd sing if she got caught. I get that she's loyal, but for a price, right? Anyway, we'll be able to figure out the rest of it once she's gone through the process. It'll remain dormant until then anyway.

Drinks on me tonight, old man. We did it!

S.

05
NOVA

This wasn't right. I wasn't supposed to be here, in this shitty bunker. I should've been with them, carrying out my mission. Buying my freedom. Not trapped here, underground with him.

He was staring at me, making sure his gaze lingered on every inch of my skin. He was good-looking, with a strong jaw and dark brown hair that matched his eyes, but the arrogant curl of his lip told me he knew it too. He found me attractive—the bulge in his trousers gave

19

him away—but his eyes weren't looking at me with desire. Far from it.

They reminded me of a nurse I'd once worked with, the kind who did our job because he liked the vulnerability of our wards. When I worked shifts after him, I would find marks that shouldn't have been there, bruises where he had no business being. I reported him once, thinking they would fire him, but they'd only transferred him to another house.

His eyes were like this man's. Heavy-lidded and dark, glittering, cruel. Like the eyes of a feral cat I'd seen at the zoo. Like he wanted to eat me, just for the fun of it.

Keep it together, Nova.

I drew my legs up to my chest, trying to cover my nakedness. Why was I naked, anyway? Last I remembered, I'd been fully clothed. With a lump in my throat, I examined my skin, looking for the telltale signs.

He laughed. "Don't worry. I didn't touch you."

"But my clothes…"

"Okay, I didn't touch you much."

"Then why take my clothes off?"

"I know who you are, what you are."

"I'm not sure what you mean." I tried to make my face look as bland as possible.

The smile spreading across his face was slow, insincere. "Sure you do. Why pretend?"

The warm blush of fear spread in the bottom of my belly. He was holding something behind his back, something heavy. I couldn't help it; my forefinger traced my thumbnail.

"I'm not pretending. Look, we need to find a way out of here. They might need our help."

"Who's they?"

"They. The people who made us, who put us here. They haven't come back for us, so obviously, they're in trouble." I spotted my clothes, only a few feet away from where I was sitting on the bed.

20

"They're not coming back. Nobody's looking for you." He rolled *his shoulders, shifting whatever he was holding from one hand to the other.*

"How do you know that?"

"I just know." His arm came out from behind his back. A *hunting knife gleamed in his hand, its back edge jagged with teeth. He wove it back and forth languorously, as though hypnotized. "What do you think hurts the most?" he asked. "When you push it in, or when you pull it out?"*

The moisture in my mouth disappeared until my tongue scraped like sandpaper. He couldn't intimidate me like this. "Would you like me to try it out on you? Then you can tell me."

His amusement was an awful choking sound. "No, I figured I'd use it on you."

I glanced involuntarily at the warped door. Damn. He'd be on me before I reached it. I didn't even think I could open it, based on the damage. Plus, I'd read about bunkers. They always had a lock, something to keep people in and everything else out. I needed to change tack. I hated what I was about to do, but I was desperate.

"Are you sure?" I asked, dropping my arms and opening my knees. "Are you sure you don't have anything else you'd like to push into me?" I pulled a long black curl of my hair between my fingers, but he wasn't looking at my face any longer. I rubbed myself, slowly at first, then faster, never taking my eyes off his face. To my surprise, I was getting wet. My scent filled the air, and when he swallowed hard, victory rushed through me, mingled with relief. It didn't last long.

When he laughed again, it had a sharp edge to it that made my teeth hurt. "Yeah," he said, "You're not really doing it for me. Smells a bit desperate."

I ignored my burning face and drew my knees up to my chest again. "Sure you don't want to finish? It'll be the last time."

The warm knot of fear in my belly blossomed upward, filling my chest and threatening to suffocate me. I couldn't help but glance at the door again, wondering how far I'd make it before he cut me down.

21

Would the nanites save me? Was I able to die? Maybe I should pretend to be dead long enough for him to leave. Then I'd heal and disappear. Maybe it wouldn't hurt too much. If only I could disconnect my mind from my body, like my patients did. I could go somewhere else while it happened.

"Stop looking at the door," he said. "You don't have to worry about it. Only one of us will be leaving. Guess which one of us it will be?"

"It is our opinion that the creation of these artilects, these intelligent machines, are a threat to our very existence. We will become obsolete not only in our own economy, but as a species. One only has to look at the Industrial Revolution to understand the potential collateral damage that we will pay with our own lives. And we recognize this instinctually. Why else would we treat androids with the contempt and hatred we do? We oppress them because we know on a primeval level that they would destroy us all if given half the chance. Let's beat them to it."

—Sarah Weiland, President of the Preserve Terra Society, 2039

06
AILITH

I was in the bed again, with the full length of Tor's body pressed against my back and his thighs curled up under mine. When he realized I was awake, he started to lift his arm from where it rested, entwined with mine. But after what I'd seen when I'd opened the front door, I'd decided to trust him, and I couldn't bear that he might leave me. I trapped his arm under my elbow. He froze for a second then relaxed, his face in my hair. It should've felt strange and awkward, but it didn't.

A tickle in my mind. *He was waiting. As always.*

We lay on top of the covers, my breathing rapid and shallow, his long and deep. Everything in me was light and temporary, like a bird ready to take flight. He listened about the woman in the bunker, the man with the knife. I didn't tell him everything; some of it seemed too private to share, like a betrayal of part of myself.

"It's not the first time I've…been her, either. What do you think it is?" I asked. "Dreams? It was like I was there, inside her, but all I could do was see and feel. I couldn't move, I couldn't speak. Her thoughts were my thoughts. It was like I became her, but I was still aware that we were two separate people. Does that make sense?"

He paused for a long time before answering. "I don't know. Maybe it's a side effect. Did you have these dreams before you became a cyborg?"

"I don't think so. I…" I tried to remember. I had trouble sometimes. The treatments that kept me alive interfered with my brain. "I'm pretty sure I didn't." I waited for him to be incredulous, to ask how I couldn't understand my own mind. But he didn't. He changed the subject instead.

He told me what had happened, what I'd seen right before I passed out. Why the air was freezing. Why there was no sun.

"All the tension that had been building between the Terrans and the Cosmists finally hit breaking point. It came out on the news that an artilect had actually been created."

"I heard about that, just before I went under. Wasn't it just a rumor?"

"It probably was. But for whatever reason, people believed it this time. They began to panic. Then the information on the Pantheon Modern Omega Project was leaked. And it…that's when the world went crazy. Anybody with cybernetics was issued with an order of removal. The military started to hunt us, the Program Omega cyborgs, down. It was difficult, of course, since we

24

look just as human as they do and Pantheon had already taken measures to hide us."

"But how did that become this? I mean, it's *barren* out there."

"I don't know who made the first strike, exactly. One day the news said it was the Russian Cosmists. The next it was the American Terrans. Even Canada was accused. I didn't think we had that kind of arsenal. Information came out, stuff we'd never heard before. Murders, sabotage, illegal weapon prototypes. The war had started long before we'd even known it was a possibility.

"The bombs fell in Canada on the third day. Major cities in every province were hit: Vancouver, Calgary, Toronto. And it wasn't just us. There were coordinated attacks all over the world. That was the last thing I heard.

"Those who still had to be cyberized were spirited away to their main compound, wherever that is. Those, like us, who'd already undergone the process were separated into pairs and hidden in bunkers all over the province. They only expected the war to last a few weeks, a month at most, and they'd planned to move us all to the compound after a week or two in hiding. To keep us safe, Pantheon Modern triggered a forced stasis program they'd planted in all the cyborgs from Program Omega."

Being put to sleep without my knowledge, even if it was for a good reason, made me sick. "And then?"

"And then…I don't know exactly. I was underground, with you."

"But you were obviously awake before me. *What happened?*"

His eyes had become glassy. "The world was…just over. While we were in the bunker, communications went down, and the earth burned. More bombs leveled entire cities and scorched the earth around them for miles. Have you heard of Russian Tar?"

"Isn't it some sort of napalm?"

"That's right. It was banned, never used, but someone, not the Russians, got the formula for it and…it clung to every surface and burned for days. There was explosive lightning, firestorms that raged unchecked.

"Many people survived the war itself. But then ash from the firestorms blocked the sun, and the temperature plummeted. People burned, and froze, and starved, and fought, and died."

"But lots of people survived, right? I mean, I know we're out in the woods, but—"

"No, Ailith. I mean, yes, people survived, but very few. The world we knew is gone."

"How do you know all this?"

"I…I talked to some survivors."

When I was ten, I'd been playing on some old farming machinery when I'd fallen and sliced my arm. There was no pain at first, just the glistening brilliance of the open wound and a terrible clarity of how bad the pain would be once it started. I'd held my breath, believing that if I didn't breathe, time wouldn't move forward, and I could stay suspended forever in that moment before the blood welled to the surface and brought agony.

All gone. My father. No. I couldn't think of him. It was too much. If I stopped to think about it, I would die. So many days had passed, over eighteen hundred of them. How many people had lived in fear before dying in fear? How many had been born into darkness? The careful hope that had taken root in me since I'd woken up was curling inwards, withering and retreating. We went so long without speaking that the fire died in the hearth. I only spoke when I had a safe question to ask. "Why are we in this house?"

"They never came back for us. After a week, I managed

to break the seal and go to the surface to have a look. I wanted to keep us moving, to keep us safe. If the wrong people had found any record of those bunkers, we'd have been sitting ducks. Plus, they were only stocked for the short-term."

Sitting ducks. Like the people who hadn't chosen a side. Who, despite their personal beliefs about artilects and cyborgs, simply wanted to live normal lives. People like my father.

I couldn't wait any longer. "I had a father," I said in a rush.

His chest expanded. "Ailith." The softness of his voice told me my father was dead.

"You don't *know*, though, do you?" How could he, when we'd slept through it?

"No, I don't. But, Ailith, it's been five years. It's... There's almost nobody left."

"Yes, but how do you *know*? Maybe it's only this part of the country. Maybe he found other survivors, and he's starting over with them."

He was silent.

I tried a different approach. "What about you? Didn't you have a family?"

"I did," he said, his voice tight. "A mother." The way he said it, I knew she was dead. But there was something else, a dullness to his tone. His grief was old, blunted. All of a sudden, I was cold. "You never talked to any survivors, did you?"

The muscles rippled in his jaw. "Yes, but—"

"Tor, how long have you been awake?"

"Ailith..." He paused. "I never went to sleep." He said it gently, as though the truth would hurt me. It did.

"Why not? Did something go wrong?"

"You were already in stasis when they took us to the

27

bunker. They said you were too important for both of us to go to sleep." He held up a hand before I could ask. "I don't know what they meant by that. They took us to the bunker and told me to stay put until they retrieved us."

For five years, he'd watched over me, a stranger, just because another stranger had told him to. He'd guarded me and waited for the end—any end—to come. *That* was why he felt so familiar. For five years, he'd protected me.

Something occurred then to me that was completely irrational, given the circumstances. *Is this the beginning of my nervous breakdown?* "You've seen me naked." It was hard to keep the accusatory tone from my voice.

A puff of air gusted against my scalp as he laughed. "Yes. I've seen you naked." I stiffened away from him, which only made his shoulders shake harder. "Look, would you rather I'd left you in the same underwear for five years?"

I couldn't argue with that.

"What did I eat? How did I go to the bathroom?"

"You didn't. Nothing went in, nothing came out. You were just…frozen. I don't even think you aged."

"So why am I awake now?"

"I don't know. About two weeks ago, you started to move. Tiny movements. A finger one day, a toe the next. Then, last week, you began having seizures. And that's when I strapped you down."

"Thank you," I whispered.

He didn't laugh again.

He pulled away from me, the mattress springing up as he stood. Cold air slammed into my back. "I need to get the fire going again."

"What did you see? For you to know what happened, what did you see?" I called after him. He didn't answer, so I followed him.

He was kneeling in front of the hearth, striking something together. He avoided my gaze.

"Are there others? Like us?"

This time he looked at me. "I have no idea. I am sure there were. As to whether there still are..."

The room began to spin again. It was too much for me to take in. What if this was a dream, like the other dreams? They were more real than this.

What do I do?

Survive, a voice inside me whispered, pushing back the part that needed to scream, to fall apart and be forever undone. I focused on Tor, the cut of his face in the glow of his fledgling fire. My hands ached to wrap themselves in his hair, to twist it around my fingers and hold together the pieces of my broken heart.

In less than a heartbeat, I was beside him. "Tor—"

He lifted his eyes to mine. Kneeling, his face was level with my stomach. I pulled him in, pressing him against me. He didn't resist, and as he wrapped his arms around me, his breath flared quick and hot through the fabric of my shirt.

I would've cried then, had there not been a sudden scratching at the door.

"Why is it that our first instinct when creating a being in our own image is to either screw it or kill it?"

—*Emily Fraser-Herondale, Of Gods and Monsters: The Rise of Artificial Intelligence*

07
ADRIAN

The day they announced the winner, I couldn't stop looking at my watch. It was going to be me. I had hoped so hard it had to happen. I wiped my slick palms on the calves of my trousers, where nobody would see.

And finally, it was time. After careful consideration and weeks of testing and observation, they'd chosen the most successful candidate for the job. And it was me; it was actually me. I couldn't believe it. I'd only been working at Pantheon Modern for three weeks when they announced the contest.

Of course, we all wanted to win it. Why else work at a corporation like Pantheon Modern if we didn't want to become cyborgs ourselves, to help usher in a new age from the front lines? The company wanted someone who would best represent them, and that person was me.

The heat from many hands burned through the thin fabric of my shirt. Everyone acted glad for me, though of course they wished they'd been chosen instead.

They gave us the rest of the day off to celebrate or commiserate. The guys were going to take me out, somewhere special. I'd heard some of them whispering about it in their cubicles when they believed no one was listening. I'd never been invited to join them until today.

It was called Pris, a place where you bought sex. And not just any sex—sex with androids. I couldn't have gone with them before, even if I'd been invited. Not on a junior exec's salary. But that night, they were treating me, no expenses spared.

We drank champagne in the limo on the way, flicking through the brothel's menu. Sid swiped through the images, barely glancing at the screen. He'd been there a few times; he was going to help me choose.

"Had her. And her. And her. And him. And him. And her."

"It might be faster if you showed him the ones you haven't had," Jal said. He was a junior like me, but his family was rich. This wasn't his first time either. "He probably doesn't want your sloppy seconds."

My face burned, but I laughed along with them. Nerves made my palms sweat again. It wasn't so much the sex; I'd had sex before. But I'd never had sex with an android. Or paid for it, for that matter.

Julie had stopped by my desk on her way out. Those who weren't coming with us wanted to have their own celebration. I'd almost wished I was going with them instead.

"Are you actually going to do it?" she'd asked.

"Do what?" I'd hoped she wasn't aware of what we were up to. I'd liked Julie ever since I'd started working at Pantheon Modern, and having the chick you liked realize you're going off to bang another one wasn't the best way to start a relationship.

"Oh, please," she'd said, her mouth twisted up on one side. "You know exactly what I mean."

"Yes." Why deny it when she already knew?

"Don't you think it's a bit wrong?"

"No. Why would it be? They're only providing a service."

"Are they? Or are they just being provided?"

I wasn't sure what she'd meant, which must've been obvious. She'd rolled her eyes and stalked off, her heels clicking angrily on the glossy floor.

I never would've guessed what Pris was from the outside; it echoed every other steel-gray granite building on the block, its name set above

31

the double-doors in wrought bronze. I studied the man on the door, trying to decide whether he was human or not.

He caught me looking and smirked. "Sorry, son, I'm not for sale."

The guys whooped with laughter.

"Don't blow your load before we even walk through the door," Sid joked.

I hadn't thought it possible to blush any harder; I was wrong.

Inside, a human hostess led us to a long couch, her red-tipped fingers gesturing with a flourish for us to sit. She bent low from the waist, her corset offering her breasts to Sid like plums on a plate as she handed him the drinks menu. Once we each had a glass in our hands, the hostess returned, leading a group of women and men dressed in lingerie. I couldn't decide if they looked more or less human than I'd imagined they would.

My drink was gone in three gulps. Another one immediately appeared in my hand, deposited by the smiling hostess. The guys were looking at the androids, discussing their different attributes with each other.

They were stunning, each one more exotic than the last. I hadn't known that women—or men, for that matter—looked like that, or smelled like that either. Their different scents mingled with each other in the air: vanilla, musk, leather. They stared straight ahead, their arms at their sides.

They were way out of my league. I wasn't bad looking, but I had a blond-haired, blue-eyed scruffy look that made me seem a lot younger than I was.

What if I couldn't get it up?

I cringed inside. I'd never live that down.

Jal elbowed me in the ribs. "You look a little worried, mate."

"No, I uh…there's so many choices."

"Look." His voice dropped to a whisper too quiet for the others to hear. "They're not alive. They're machines. I know they look human, but it's an illusion. Look closer. They're basically glorified *sex dolls. Don't worry about it."*

I took his advice and scrutinized them. Jal was right. They stood stiffly, unmoving and unblinking. Everything about them was too perfect. I searched for a hint of resentment on their faces and found nothing but the blankness of a machine.

I could do this.

"Hurry up and choose already. The rest of us are waiting."

I called the hostess over, then pointed to a woman on the far right. She was attractive, but not inaccessibly so. She had a kind of girl-next-door look. In fact, she resembled Julie, with her long red hair and a smattering of freckles on her pearly skin. Her body was petite, her breasts small and pointed through the gauzy film of jade chiffon.

When I got closer to her, I caught a trace of antiseptic under her apple-pie scent, which almost made me lose my nerve. She led me down the unadorned hallway and into a room, where she closed the door behind us. The room was decorated to complement her, a young woman's bedroom: ivory and sea-green wallpaper, mounds of pillows, a vanity with a variety of powders and perfumes. How much of it was for show? I pictured her sitting on the small stool, combing her hair, looking anxiously in the mirror to make sure her makeup was just right.

"Do you sleep here?" I asked her. No one had ever accused me of being an impressive conversationalist.

"You are very handsome," she replied, ignoring my question.

"Uh…thanks. You too. I mean, you're very beautiful."

"Would you like me to take my clothes off?" She pinched the ribbons of her negligee between her flawlessly manicured fingers.

"Don't you want to talk a bit first? What's your name?"

"Do you not like me?"

"What? Yes, of course, I do. I just—"

"Do you want me to take my clothes off?" Her guileless green eyes were wide.

"Um, ok. Yes, please."

She watched my face as she untied her translucent robe and let it

33

slip from her shoulders to the floor.

Her body was symmetrical, with none of the imperfections of the women I'd been with before, who always seemed to have one breast larger than the other, or a mole in an awkward place. She was smooth and completely hairless except for her neatly trimmed triangle.

"Do you want me to take your clothes off?" she inquired.

"No. No, I can do it myself, thank you."

"You're welcome."

I stripped, fumbling with the buttons on my shirt. Usually, when I found myself in this situation, I was clumsy because I was rushing and trying to make out with the girl at the same time, unable to keep my hands off her. Her arms remained stiffly at her sides. Once I was naked, we stood facing each other.

"What would you like me to do?" she asked.

"I, uh, what would you like to do?"

"I would like to please you."

I didn't know what to say. Somehow, the idea of asking her to drop to her knees and suck me off seemed degrading.

"Lie down on the bed, I guess."

She followed my instructions, lying down in the center of the generous mattress. "Like this?"

"Yes." I was growing hard at the sight of her now, lying on the silky sheets, waiting for me. Willing to do whatever I wanted. And right then, I wanted to celebrate. No pretenses. It was all about me.

"Spread your legs," I commanded, and she did.

After I was done, I pulled out of her, not looking at the mess I'd made. I wasn't sure whether to cuddle her or not. She got off the bed and stood in the center of the room, my semen smeared down one of her thighs.

"Was I satisfactory?" she asked.

"Yes, thank you. Was it okay for you?"

"You are very handsome," she repeated and blinked.

"The only way to ensure, beyond a doubt, that our species will survive is to propagate ourselves into a form that's more capable of adapting, of surviving, than ourselves. As a species, we've already reached our full potential. Our constant need to war over resources and religion, our inability to extend to all members of our own species even the most basic right to life, and the means by which to support that life, proves that our time as a flourishing species is over."

—Robin Leung, CEO of Novus Corporation, 2039

08

AILITH

The knife left his hand before I even knew he'd lifted it. End over end it spun, faster than a human eye could see, than a human arm could throw, a dark blur through the gray air. The knife caught me off guard; he normally wielded a crossbow. His breath slid up the bare skin of my neck, causing a ripple down my spine. My pants were crisp with the cold, but I was too wired with anticipation to feel the chill.

His knife skewered the hare through the heart, pinning it to the ground. I finally exhaled. We'd been kneeling in the skeletal forest for hours, waiting for something edible to walk by. The waiting itself was boring, since Tor wasn't the talkative type, but there wasn't much else to do. He didn't want me exploring on my own, and I had too much sense to rebel for the sake of it—although, if I was being honest, it was because I was afraid of what I might see.

The blood reminded me of the last vision I'd had, the cascade of crimson hair down her back. It hadn't hit me as hard as the others. I hadn't gone blind, at least. Whatever the visions were, I was beginning to gain some control over them.

What are they? I tried not to think of the vacancy on the android's face as I thrust myself into her, over and over, her hair rasping against the brocade pillow. Since then, I'd caught only wisps of images from the threads, like seeing something on the edge of my vision, only for it to be gone when I finally looked.

"Remind me where we are, again," I asked as he brushed past me to retrieve the warm body of the hare, his breath cloudy in the cold air.

"The Kootenays."

It was warmer today than it had been since I'd woken up just over a week ago, but the mountain air was still biting. I couldn't remember if I'd ever been to the Kootenays before.

"Okay, but *where* in the Kootenays?"

Tor paused, chewing on his lower lip. "The map says we're near a city called Redcot. Ever been there?"

"No. You?"

"Nope. I'd never gone farther than the Lower Mainland. I guess that's one good thing about the apocalypse: it's gotten me to travel."

Tor's plan was for us to stay put for the next few weeks, and then...then we'd see. He was determined to avoid other people as much as possible. He wouldn't say why, only that people had, and yet hadn't, changed since the war. If what he'd told me was true, the risk of others finding us was small. Still, he wanted to be cautious.

We'd settled into a comfortable routine that centered

around finding things to eat, and eating them, something I needed to do now that I was awake. I'd also found some books under the layers of dust as we'd made ourselves at home and had taken to reading aloud to Tor in the evenings, cross-legged and squinting in front of the fire.

I wasn't as keen to stay here as he was. Though it was unlikely, a small part of me wondered if my father could still be alive. But we were far from where I'd lived in the Okanagan in the south of the province, and I wasn't ready to make that journey myself. I was sure that, given a bit more time, I could convince Tor to come with me.

Though technically the end of spring, it was only a handful of degrees above freezing, the ground rock-hard under its delicate carpet of evergreen needles. I wasn't used to living in the mountains. Although they shared the same fir and pine trees, they were a far cry from the beaches and vineyards I'd grown up with.

"So, it just got colder after the war?" I asked him.

"Yes. It happened so gradually I assumed it was just the changing of the seasons. But it kept getting colder and never really warmed up again. That's when the plants and animals started dying, and most of the remaining survivors followed them."

"I still don't understand how that many people could've died."

"There was something else in those bombs. Something that made people sick. Many of those who didn't die in the war were killed by whatever it was. There were weeks of silver rain, and… Well, it doesn't matter. That silver rain rarely falls any more, and it's starting to get warmer. It's warmer now than it was this time last year.

"Take these hares, for example. They're a good sign. For the first year or two after it got really cold, I didn't see any living animals, only acres of untouched carcasses just frozen in time. Even the birds had gone silent. They've started to appear again, like the animals, although they're not the same ones as before. All the wildlife here now seems to have migrated from the north. I guess it's more of their usual climate down here. The predators have begun to recover as well, but it'll be a long time before they're hungry enough to find us interesting."

He grinned and held up the hare for me to admire before adding it to the rest. Unruly black hair curled over his pale face and neck, blending with the inky lines of his tattoos. His eyes were always dark, but now they held a fierce glint that was unrelated to the brightness of his smile. I had quickly learned that such smiles were rare for Tor, his mouth naturally downcast. The strings of hares rode his shoulders like wings, forming a dark tableau against the naked trees. A whisper of fear brushed my mind, too delicate to grasp.

I suddenly realized that he was speaking to me, and the whisper vanished.

"Sorry, what?"

"I said, are you ready to go back now?"

"How many do we have?" I asked. He was too polite to point out the wrongness of *we*, since he'd done all the actual killing.

"Eight, all together." His quiet voice carried over the still air as he stretched his shoulders, the strings of hares twisting in a macabre dance.

"Eight is a respectable number," I said, trying to sound casual. I didn't want to seem too eager to get back. He thought I enjoyed the hunting, and I didn't want to hurt his feelings. Besides, I liked watching *him* hunt.

He adjusted the hares and retraced our steps to the cottage. I walked beside him, admiring his grace from the corner of my eye. I'd had an appreciation for Tor's body ever since we'd heard the scratching outside the door that first night.

The speed and silence with which he'd moved had made my breath catch much more than my fear of what was on the other side. It had been nothing but a curious fox, but it had made me think. Despite everything I'd learned in the short time I'd been awake, I hadn't given much consideration to how the cyberization had changed us. It wasn't like we'd been left with an instruction manual. Yes, we were stronger and healed faster, but surely there had to be more?

I was curious how different Tor was now to when he'd been an ordinary human, but I wasn't quite sure how to ask. He wasn't the same Tor who'd held me that first night. After the incident with the fox, the easy intimacy had disappeared, reminding me how little I knew about him. I was desperate to ask him more about the war, but so far, he hadn't been particularly forthcoming.

"So, you're pretty good with that crossbow. Did you do a lot of hunting before the war?"

"Not animals," he replied.

Okay... "And the gathering?" Earlier that morning, he'd shown me some edible plants he'd found.

He leaned over to peer at a small thorned bush. "I've poisoned myself a few times figuring it out, but because of the nanites, all I got was a bit of a stomachache." He wiped his forehead with the back of his hand, marring the clean lines of his tattoos with hare blood.

"What do the designs on your face mean?" I was fascinated by the intricate pattern. Two sets of three lines curved upward across his forehead, intersecting in the middle. They swept down over his temples and converged into a single stripe on either side of his face, ending at his jawline. Delicate branches twined out from each central

39

stroke, one flowing into each corner of his eyes, the other into his hairline. A thicker line slid vertically over his lower lip and down his chin, where the branching pattern repeated on his throat. They were striking and oddly familiar, but I couldn't begin to place them.

"They're a warning." His eyes were darker, and he said nothing more.

I had stooped to gather some pale-yellow berries Tor swore were safe to eat when it hit me; a shift in my awareness. The voice inside me whispered, "*Here it comes.*" There was a tugging on my spine, a stiffening, as though I were a puppet and someone had suddenly pulled hard on my strings. At first, I couldn't feel the ground beneath me, like I was flying, but I wasn't; I was on my knees. Time had stopped, and my voice caught in my throat.

Whatever had happened to me also happened to Tor, but his reactions were far faster than mine, and he'd made it to within a few feet of me, his fingers grasping at the empty air. We stared at each other, and I saw my reflection in his eyes—a pale face peering out of a black well.

We were frozen for what seemed like hours, but when we finally fell, the body of the last hare was still warm. We lay there, face-to-face.

"Tor? Are you okay?" I asked when I was finally able to speak. "What *was* that?"

He winced as he lifted his head from the ground, and there were bloody scratches along his cheek. "I have no idea. I—"

It came again. The pull, the voice. Wanting us to leave this place, to come…*home*. I whispered his name.

"We have to get home." His voice was shaky as he jerked me to my feet. "Now."

"But we don't know where home is."

"I mean home. *Our* home."

40

The word *our* in his mouth moved something in my chest. "Tor."

"No." He walked off, staggering slightly over the rough ground.

I had no choice but to follow.

"I do not think you understand the gravity of what you are proposing. You are not talking about simply integrating these people with biomechatronic components. You are talking about combining every human cell in their bodies with robotic elements. Not only are you creating virtually immortal beings, you cannot accurately predict what enhancements will result, or what they will become capable of."

—*Sarah Weiland of the Preserve Terra Society at the Pantheon Modern Cyborg Symposium, 2040*

09
TOR

The blood on my knuckles was already starting to dry; the cuts from his broken teeth would take longer to heal. His eyes had held the same look as all the others: confusion then comprehension then fear. He hadn't begged or tried to bargain. Not all of them did. But he would remember my face. Even without my tattoos, he would remember. It was, after all, the last thing he would see.

Bile burned the back of my throat. The first few times, I'd thrown up. Not now. Footsteps echoed on the tiles in the hallway, and it became difficult to breathe. I ran my fingers through my hair, trying to tame it, then immediately hated myself. What did I care how she saw me? She didn't. All she cared about was owning me.

She opened the door gently, hoping to surprise me, to catch me off my guard. She wasn't aware that I always smelled her long before she came into the room—her cloying perfume of violets and balsam, a sickly-sweet scent that did nothing to cover the odor of decay. The drug was eating her from the inside out, and no perfume in her arsenal could hide it from me. I only wished she would hurry up and die. Then I could stop loving her.

I didn't flinch as she laid her hand on my shoulder.

"Did you know you have blood in your hair?" she asked, digging her fingers into my skin.

I kept my eyes on my hands.

"Look at me." She said my name, the sound of it painful to my ears.

I looked, unable to stop myself.

She appeared to be well today, younger, almost like when we first met. Her face was pale and smooth, akin to the antique dolls my mother used to keep on a shelf in the guest room. Her hair was as black as mine, but straight and silky, and cut into a severe bob that framed her delicate face. She stroked my cheek, her acrylic nails making a dry scraping sound that made me want to put my hands on her with violence.

It was difficult for her to be so gentle; it wasn't her nature. In her defense, it wasn't entirely her fault. She'd grown up in this life. I hadn't. Her only way out was death, as was mine—at least until a few weeks ago. And it was she who'd unwittingly given me the key.

She slid into my lap and moved against me in gentle circles. It was what she did whenever she thought I was angry at her, and when I hardened in spite of myself, she couldn't suppress the victory in her slanted blue eyes. That was her power, the reason she existed. We were both pets, no matter how hard she pretended she wasn't.

Her father was our keeper, and she, his faultless creation. I was also what he'd made me, but I'd had a choice. In deciding to be with her, I'd embraced this life, as he'd known I would. As she'd known I would. My mother had tried so hard to keep me from people like them, had sacrificed so much. And yet, here I was.

She traced her fingers over the splits in my skin. "What was it this time? Debt? Reneged on a deal? Chose the wrong wine at supper?"

43

"Do you really care?" It was impossible to keep the harshness out of my voice.

Her eyes narrowed.

I needed to stop rebelling and just play along. She'd been spying on me, showing up unexpectedly. She'd also been poking around in my room, the haze of drugs making her less careful than she'd thought. It was as though she knew something had changed, but her mind couldn't focus long enough to figure it out.

"Sorry," I said. "I'm just tired. He was the third one this week."

"You're supposed to be resting." She studied my face.

"I know. But an order's an order, right?"

She pouted up at me, a look that used to tie my stomach up in knots with anticipation. Now, it merely made it churn. I knew what she truly was, the sickness in her. I'd missed it before, those few years ago, under the layers of her makeup and my own infatuation. She was now a caricature of that woman, the softness replaced by something cold, and dazzling, and rotten.

Two weeks. Two more weeks, and I'd be free. God knew how high up her father's boss was on the food chain, but he was well-placed enough to have me pushed to the front of the line for the Pantheon Modern cyborg program. Such was the truth of my position. I was important enough for the syndicate to invest in me, but expendable enough to be replaced if I died during the process. It was true that a machine could do my job, but then, a machine didn't have my flaws. A machine would be difficult to bend without breaking.

If I did survive, I'd have to disappear. The violence I was currently capable of would be insignificant in comparison. And yet, I'd have less power than I did now.

She wriggled in my lap, having noticed that my attention was elsewhere. I fought the urge to push her off, to strike her. She smiled at me, running her tongue across her teeth. I swallowed hard, trying not to retch. She misinterpreted my reaction and ground against me before rubbing a finger over her bottom lip and smearing her chin with red.

44

Two weeks.

I turned my head away as she dropped to her knees and licked the blood from my hands.

We've activated the homing signal. Lexa wanted to do it earlier. She's worried they might be in trouble. I'm sure they can handle themselves, although, if I'm honest, it's more than that. Lexa may look upon them as children, assuming they'll love her simply because she's their mother. I'm not so sure. She's worried about protecting them; I'm worried about protecting us. Who knows how they'll react? They're waking up to an unfamiliar world, and even their own bodies and minds will be as unknown to them as they are to us. How much of them will have changed? The process is unpredictable at best, and dangerous at worst. And we rushed it, damn us. It was more important to prove that we could do it than consider what it would do to them.

—Mil Cothi, *personal journal; June 5th, 2045*

10

AILITH

My head was tender. The threads had blazed again during the night, more intensely. More *real*. Rather than lie awake staring into the darkness, curiosity had gotten the better of me, and I'd decided to go exploring. I was drawn to this latest thread by the brilliance of its connection to me.

I still smelled the fetid sweetness of her breath, was both repulsed and aroused by her hands on me, her mouth as she took me inside it. I had again been a man, my body well-built and powerful. My arms were crisscrossed with scars of all different ages, the bloody cuts on my hands fresh. I'd been desperate to escape; it had taken everything in my power not to grab her and break her over my knee. But there'd also been a hope deep inside me that helped me bear it, tiny tendrils blooming and curling around my ribs.

A storm raged outside, and the sturdy walls of our house creaked in disapproval. I got out of bed and glanced at myself in the mirror. It wasn't functioning, of course; all I saw was my reflection. I didn't mind. The last thing I needed right now was a smug voice helpfully suggesting which creams to apply so I looked less crap.

Seeing myself was odd. My face was no longer my own. It was the same face I'd always had, but when I studied myself in the mirror, it was like I was wearing a mask. Even the touch of my own hand didn't feel right. An otherness lived within my body, which I assumed must be the nanites. Far away, the voice inside me laughed.

Tor stood behind me in the door frame. He was surprisingly alert. I'd heard him pacing the floor of his bedroom every time I'd woken during the night. We hadn't spoken about what had happened. Did he still sense it? The need to leave, to find where the voice would lead us?

"Good morning."

"Morning." We were formal, stiff.

"How's your—"

The scratches on his face were nearly gone; thin silvery lines were all that remained. He put his hand to his cheek and smiled. "Gotta be some perks to being a monster, right?"

"Is that how you feel? That you're a monster?"

"Sometimes." He said it as though it were a joke, but I wasn't so sure. He must've felt the otherness too. We'd spent the last week avoiding discussing what we were, or where we were from. All we'd talked about was the

47

weather, food, and how best to clean the house.

He had a fire burning in the living room. The house seemed more like a home now, *our home*, as he'd said yesterday. Cleaning had done nothing to improve the pale chartreuse of the walls, but at least the surfaces were no longer covered in dust. The furnishings were sparse, whether due to the aesthetic taste of the previous owner or looting, I had no idea. None of the house functions worked without electricity, of course, but we were managing.

I curled up on our lone couch and pressed the heels of my palms into my eye sockets, trying to dull the aching in my head.

"Are you okay?" Tor asked, frowning.

"Yeah, it's only a headache. I had another vision. An intense one. It's funny. Some of them seem to be from the past, like memories. Others seem to be later, after the war. Maybe even the present. This latest one felt like the past. To the person I was in, life felt normal."

"Want to talk about it?" He gestured to the window. "It's not like we're going anywhere today. And there's nothing good on TV."

"Did you actually make a joke?" I asked, getting nothing but raised eyebrows in return. "Um, okay. Where do you want me to start?"

He lowered himself onto the cushion next to me and leaned forward. "Tell me what happened in the latest one."

I picked at a crack in the leather of the couch and told him about my hands, the pain of my torn skin. The sharpness of her nails, my loathing for both of us as I came. By the time I was done, he'd gone rigid.

"Who are you?" his voice was savage, a growl between clenched teeth.

"What? What do you mean?"

"Who. Are. You?" Each word was a feral bite.

"Tor, I—"

He advanced on me, his chest heaving. I had only a split second for fear before he wrapped his hands around my neck.

"…I don't have to tell you that I don't like this. As far as I'm concerned, the risk is too significant, not only of our exposure but of the end result. He is impulsive, reckless, and has a Machiavellian streak to rival my mother-in-law's. We've basically just handed a toddler a machine gun. Do you really think he's not going to pull the trigger?"

— [■■■■■■■■■■■■■■■■■■]

II
OLIVER

It was agonizing. They'd never told me it would be so goddamn painful. Every cell in my body felt like it was splitting, and I guessed, in a way, they were. The nanites were inside me, invading me, eating me alive. They were tearing me apart with their tiny claws, consuming me, spitting me out, rebuilding me.

Am I going to die?

The thought didn't scare me. It pissed me off. This was my last chance to be accepted, to assume my rightful place, even though they thought I wasn't worthy enough.

A ghost was in my brain. It was me. The ghost was cackling. If I could've gotten hold of him, I'd have torn him apart, but every time I tried, they knocked me out. They said I would need my eyes to see. No fucking kidding.

Someone lit me on fire. My body bent, my bones cracked. I wanted to laugh, to show them my strength, but I forgot where my mouth was. Skin tore underneath my fingernails, bunching in ribbons and falling to the floor.

This had better be worth it. I'd better get what they've promised me. All my life I'd wanted to be one of them. But only now, in the eleventh hour, were they desperate enough to use me. But they would see my worth. I'd make them. And they'd give me what was owed.

I had debased myself for them, for us all. Together, we would level the playing field. I would give them their future, and they would give me what I deserved. They couldn't refuse me after this. No. They would celebrate me almost as much as what was to come.

This was my last chance, but it was also theirs.

I was their savior, and if they tried to crucify me this time, I would end them.

"Who are they to tell us what we can and cannot do with our own bodies? It's not just about becoming faster, stronger, or smarter. For the chronically ill, it's about having a reasonable quality of life. And for the terminally ill, it's literally a matter of life and death. Complete cyberization would give us the ability to transcend the prisons of our damaged and dying bodies. Who are the Terrans and the Cosmists to tell me I cannot, while they themselves not only get to live the way they choose, but to live?"

—Dolan Smythe, advocate; *Cyborgs for Life*, 2040

12

AILITH

I hadn't meant to follow that thread. It was a reflex, an escape. One I regretted. My fingers itched, desperate to claw at my eyes. Now I was aware again, although I was no longer sure what was real. Was Tor a vision? No. His hands were around my neck, the empty air beneath my feet.

We both panted: me gasping for air, him from rage and fear. He held me pinned against the wall, his knee between my legs. Bloody tracks raked his face, and something sticky covered my fingernails.

Within the expanding brown and gold pleats of his irises, I saw them. The nanites, millions of tiny machines propelled by gilded filaments toward the black pinprick of his pupil. As they converged in the center, his iris overflowed, and the nanites streamed down his face in veins of precious metal.

I'm hallucinating.

Even when he was trying to kill me, he was beautiful. Especially when. I had the sudden wild urge to kiss him, to touch the lips that were pulled back from his teeth and run my fingers over the cut stone of his face. Hysteria tried to force its way out of my throat and managed only a pathetic gurgle.

His eyes were clear. He saw me, every inch of me, and in that moment, I understood that I didn't know him at all. Darkness frayed the edges of my vision. I wanted to fight back, but I had nothing left. Whatever gifts my transformation had given me, the physical strength to rival his wasn't one of them.

He pulled me forward then slammed me back again, smashing my spine against the hard plaster. The third time, something gave way.

I traced my finger down the tattoo on his lower lip. His skin was firm and smooth, marred only by a faint scar through the left side of his mouth.

Do I have enough strength for one last attack?

Air, tasting of smoke and blood, rushed into my lungs.

I was still pinned to the wall, but he'd dropped his hands from my throat to my shoulders. He held them gently, although his breath was still coming fast. He leaned his forehead against mine as he fought for control.

I didn't want to move too quickly for fear of reigniting him. I crept my fingers up the side of his face again, and he broke, dropping to his knees. Without the support, I slid to the ground. My legs were unfeeling, unmoving, and I suspected he'd broken something in my back.

He tightened his fingers on my shoulders, and I winced, afraid we were going to start all over again. He yanked his hands from me and clenched them uncertainly before pressing them against the floor.

"Ailith." He spoke with something deeper than regret. "Ailith, I'm sorry, I—"

I couldn't stop touching his face. I needed to feel him. That damned voice whispered in my ear, *"Always."* If I'd been able to lean forward, I would've kissed him. *I've finally lost my mind.*

"Tor?"

"What are you?" he asked again, softly this time.

"I-I'm not sure what you mean."

He searched my face. Whatever he saw knocked the air out of him but saved me. "That vision you had, the last one. It was me."

"What do you mean, it was you?"

"I mean, it was *me*. That happened *to me*. What you...saw. It was real. *She* was real. That was my life...before."

My stomach went cold, the white kind of chill that had filled it when the doctors told me that, despite all their technology, there was nothing else they could do for me. The iciness was a spike, trying to pierce its way beyond my stomach and out through my mouth.

I recalled the hollowness of being inside him, the emptiness. I couldn't reconcile that with the Tor I knew, but now, with his wildness unbound, I caught a glimpse of that former man, and my heart hurt for him.

He released my shoulders, and I slumped onto the floor. The solid hardness of the wood was soothing, although from that angle, I noticed some dust balls I'd missed under the couch.

"I'm sorry," he said again.

"It's okay." I was shocked at my own calmness, although I flinched when he raised a hand toward me.

His face blanched. "Ailith, please. Let's get off this

54

floor. We need to talk."

"I can't. I think you cracked something." I was still trying to swallow around the thickness in my throat.

The color drained from his face, his tattoos standing out in vivid detail. "I— Oh, Ailith."

"Tor, it's okay. It won't last. Give me a few minutes." The nanites tingled inside me, at work repairing the damage. "Look." I wiggled my toes to show him. Only, they didn't actually move. "Okay, I might need more than a few minutes. I don't think it's actually *broken*, just a bit cracked."

"Does it hurt?" His voice caught. "I didn't mean—"

"Yes, you did. You did mean it. Maybe not to hurt me this badly, but you wanted to hurt me. But I get it. I probably would've reacted the same. Not that I'd do too much damage to you with this body." I hoped my smile was convincing.

"I believe your body could do me a lot of damage," he muttered under his breath.

"What?"

He rocked onto his heels and stood. "I'll be right back."

He returned a few minutes later with a pillow and some blankets. After he'd tucked the blankets around me, he placed the pillow on his lap and gently eased my head on to it. The prickling of so many nanites at work made me want to throw up. Did all of them come running in an emergency like this? It felt like it. I needed some distraction.

"What did you mean, it was your life, before?"

He stiffened. "Before the war, I was an enforcer for a syndicate."

"Who was she? That girl, the one you…"

He took a deep breath. "No one."

"She didn't seem like no one." His teeth were grinding

55

against each other. *Should I let it go?*

He didn't answer for a long time. When he did, his words were a mix of resentment and sadness. "She was my boss's daughter. The reason I got involved with the syndicate in the first place. We met in high school. When we began dating, he offered me the position working for him."

I remembered his loathing and anger. "You loved her?"

"Yes, very much. At first. But then... Eventually, I ended up hating her as much as I loved her. As I'm sure you felt." His voice was tight, and I didn't blame him. I wouldn't want someone to be able to see into my head either. I wanted to ask him more about her because I wanted to hate her too, but I had the feeling that line of questioning would shut him down.

"Your tattoos?"

"Yes. I got them from the syndicate. They're how people identified me. The first time they saw me was a warning. The second... I've done terrible things." In his voice were a thousand disturbing memories.

"Is that why you became a cyborg?" My throat was better now. I sounded almost human.

"Yes. I believed it would be my way out. They planned to still use me against their enemies, but I was going to take my mother and run. Then, the war happened."

"And we were taken to the bunker?"

"Yes."

"How...how do you know that your mother is dead?" I was hoping he'd only made an educated guess. If he wasn't sure, there was a chance my father was still alive.

"I went to find her. She lived near the harbor in Vancouver. Parts of it were still burning when I arrived. Can you believe that?"

I caught a flicker in my mind: asphalt like lava;

56

mountains of twisted metal and glass. Ash. Unbearable heat. Nothing was where it was supposed to be, not even the bones.

"You left me alone to go find her? On the coast? That would've taken you weeks! And you left me…" I pictured myself, asleep and vulnerable. Then, I was ashamed. "Sorry, I—"

He raised his hand, his fingers spread. "Five days, to be exact. Geographically, we were closer than we are now, somewhere near Aelshore. Since vehicles stopped working when the satellites went down, I had to walk nearly eighteen hours a day. Good thing we're faster now. I didn't know you. I didn't… Well, anyway, I made sure the entrance was invisible. The bunker was built to be a secret." He changed the subject. "Where was your father when…everything happened?"

"I assume he was at home on the farm, near Goldnesse. Did you… I mean, was Goldnesse still there?"

His lips made a thin line. "Not most of it. And that was a long time ago."

My stomach twisted. "I—We weren't on speaking terms. He didn't approve of the Pantheon Modern program. Staunch Terran, my father. He was able to pretend he was fine about it up until the night before I went in. Then he let me know how he really felt." I tried to smile, but it came out a grimace.

"But weren't you going to die without it?"

"Yes, but—"

"But what? He wanted you to die?" His voice was raised, his lip curled in disgust.

"No, of course not!" Although I wasn't sure that was the truth, I needed to defend him. No matter what may have happened toward the end, he was still my father. Or had been. "It's complicated."

"Doesn't sound complicated."

"Well, it was." My back felt healed now, if a bit weak. I was fairly certain I could sit up, but despite the uncomfortable conversation, I was more at ease than I'd been since I woke. I found being near him soothing, touching him, more so.

I gave my toes an experimental wiggle. Good as new. Propping myself up, I regarded him. "How long did it take you to get used to that? To the healing?"

"Only a few weeks. They showed me when I came out of the procedure, so I knew what to expect. Kind of. I did think it would be even faster, instantaneous, like you used to see on TV. But still, it's pretty useful."

"I'll say. Lucky for you or you'd have to carry me around with you forever."

"Ailith—" He reached out and cupped my cheek, running his thumb over my cheekbone.

The other voice inside me arched its back and purred.

"Sorry, it was a joke," I blurted. *Shut up, Ailith.*

He dropped his hand. "I'd better go see to the fire."

Damn.

He helped me stand, but as he stepped away, my legs gave out. Thanks to that inhuman speed, he managed to scoop me up before I hit the floor. As he carried me to the couch, the pulse in his neck beat rapidly against my temple, giving him away. He laid me down so gently I wanted to cry.

I finally asked the question I was sure had also been on his mind. "Tor, if what I saw was one of your memories, then what about the others? What if they're also memories? What if it's another cyborg super-power, like the strength and the healing?"

Comprehension dawned on his face.

"And if they *are* memories, *whose* memories are they?"

58

"If you are, on one hand, augmenting humans with mechanical components at the cellular level, and on the other, augmenting robots with biological components at their cellular level, where does the separation exist? At what point does one become human or machine? If they are created in the same way, are they not then, at every level, the same?"

—Della van Natta, *Artificial Life or Artificial Hope?*

13

PAX

Cindra kept apologizing to me. She was sorry she'd gotten us into our current situation; it was her fault the Terrans had captured us. I should've told her it wasn't—it was mine—but I didn't want her to be mad at me. Not right now, anyway. There would be time for that later. If she knew I'd let it happen, she would be angry.

It was kind of her fault anyway. She was the one who'd wanted to stop and help them. But I'd known they would discover what we were. I'd known they would take us. I should've taken better care to keep us hidden. But once they'd seen us, there was only one way to stay on the path we needed to take. It was our best hope for the future.

I would explain everything to her soon, when we were safe. She would forgive me. She would be happy because we'd have found Ailith. They would love each other like sisters, so she couldn't be mad.

It was going to hurt. I'd tried to convince them that the nanites only worked on us, that if they tried to use them, they would die. Cindra should never have told them what we were. It wasn't her fault, though. They'd tricked her. She'd only wanted to help them. She'd assumed that, after everything that had happened, our differences wouldn't matter anymore.

They'd known right away that we were different. Our skin was smooth, free of the damage they themselves had suffered—and, man, had they suffered.

And, of course, there was my eyes.

The whites had been jet-black ever since I'd become a cyborg, and they'd given us away.

Would they have treated us better if we'd appeared less human? Or at the very least, less perfectly human? Maybe if we'd been wearing coats. They should've left us coats in the bunker, even if it had been the middle of summer.

Cindra had been very upset when the Terrans told her about the war. Five years was a long time. Especially when you woke up and everyone was gone. I didn't mind as much.

I'd wanted us to follow the signal, the one triggered after we'd left the bunker, right on time. Cindra had wanted to go in another direction, to another home, but I'd convinced her we needed to follow what was pulling at us. It was a homing signal. We were being assembled. I was sure of it. We needed to find the source so things could begin. Otherwise, everything that had happened would have been for nothing. We needed to stay on this path to achieve the best possible outcome.

The Terrans were going to take our nanites; I'd heard them talking. They would start today, when they'd decided how to keep them working. They didn't believe me when I'd told them they would die. I didn't want the Terrans to die because then they would kill us. We needed to stay alive. We had a purpose.

Cindra was crying again, about someone called Asche. I wanted to comfort her, so I stroked her hair. My mother had liked it when I stroked her hair. It made Cindra cry harder, but she didn't want me to stop. I sang to her; my mother had liked that too.

They told me to stop singing because it was making some of the children cry. They must've been born after the war. What did they

60

think of us? Did they know about the sun? I had never thought much about it until it was gone.

They cut my arm and watched the blood closely as it dripped into the basin, trying to see the nanites. When I laughed, it made them angry. They saw the cut slowly close and assumed the nanites would heal them the same way.

The women stared at Cindra, touching their own faces and hair. They were jealous of her exotic tawny skin, her firmness, her muscles that were from health, rather than utility. I could tell they wanted to cut off her long, silky hair so the men wouldn't like her more than them. One of them spat at her. They pretended it was because she was a cyborg.

The men weren't jealous of me. They believed I was weak, and I had to let them think they were right. They'd decided that cuts were one thing to fix, broken bones another. They wondered just how much we could heal. I had to let them. Now was not the time to be who we were.

I—

Hello, Ailith. I've been waiting for you. I'm Pax. Have you been there, inside me, for long?

Please, ignore me if I scream.

"When you begin to combine man with machine, surely that is tantamount to you handing them a slice of ambrosia and saying, "here, now you are as God?"

—Sarah Weiland, President of the Preserve Terra Society, 2039

14

AILITH

Please, ignore me if I scream.

"Tor!" I shouldn't have been yelling. Someone could've heard me and come looking for us, but I didn't know what else to do. He'd gone off hunting by himself. We'd been awkward around each other all morning, avoiding eye contact and answering with only single words. Part of it was the tension that had lain thickly between us since yesterday, and part was the desire to leave. Well, my desire anyway.

Though Tor felt the pull as keenly as I did, he was suspicious of it. I wanted to follow it. Tor suspected it was a trap, and I didn't blame him. In fact, a small part of me agreed. But what if it wasn't? I wouldn't admit it to him, but another part of me wondered if my father was at the end of it, that it was his way of trying to find me. And if not that, what if others like us were there? In a safe place? It was getting harder for me to ignore.

"Tor!" Where was he? He wouldn't have gone far. He wouldn't have left me. Would he? "Tor!" My throat was beginning to ache in the cold.

He came then, flying through the woods on the far side of the clearing. He'd left everything he'd been carrying behind. As he got closer, I expected to hear the snapping of dead wood and the crunching of frozen leaves, but the air around him was impossibly silent.

He slowed to a swift walk when he saw me. Slow, steady breaths wreathed his face in the cold air. He pushed his hair back from his forehead as he peered around me. "Ailith?"

"Tor, he *talked* to me. He said my *name*. He said his name was Pax. He knew I was *there*."

His hand froze midair, snarls of hair sticking up between his fingers. "What are you saying? Someone spoke to you? In a memory?"

"I'm saying that this wasn't a memory, Tor! There's a woman named Cindra with him. They're being held captive. What's happening to them is happening right now."

"How can you know that?"

"He *spoke* to me. He knew about what happened to us the other day. It happened to them too. He called it a homing signal." The heat rose in my face. "Tor, we have to go and find them."

"Can you talk to him now?"

"I don't know." It hadn't occurred to me to try to contact whomever the memories, or whatever they were, belonged to. I'd considered them something that was happening *to* me, not *by* me. I reached out with my mind, trying to find the thread that led to him. Nothing. "I think he's unconscious. I can't...it's like he's present, but not."

"Ailith, look, if what you're saying is true—" He held up a hand as I began to protest. "What I mean is that we're not sure what these visions are. It might be a lure, Ailith,

63

like that damned...homing signal. And if what you're seeing is true, and it's happening right now, we can't simply go running into the middle of an army of Terrans. You do remember who the Terrans are, right? People who want you dead solely because you exist. Look around you! They did this. We have no idea who this Pax is, except that he's with them."

"Tor, they're being *tortured*. We can't abandon them. They're like us."

"You don't *know* that. You don't know who they are, or what's happening. You can't trust this."

I felt small and impotent. And pissed off. I closed my eyes to concentrate. My mind was a field of darkness; I waited until I spotted it at last, a slender golden thread. I slid along it until, suddenly, I was looking at myself through his eyes.

At first I was surprised: Tor saw me differently than I saw myself. I was a precious thing he wanted to keep safe. He *needed* to keep me safe; I stood between him and a precipice. Light coiled around me, solid and powerful. His feelings toward me were mixed: fear, longing, desire; something unfurling itself to the sun.

"*Tor?*" He didn't respond. The fear in his mind was growing, the thread becoming brittle and cold. He felt me inside him, and he was losing control.

"Stop!" he shouted.

Suddenly, I was back inside myself.

He stared at me with wild eyes. "Stop," he said again, quieter. He pivoted on his heel and walked away.

"Tor! I'm sorry."

He spun and came back toward me, seeming to grow larger with each step. "Never do that again." He was flushed, his hands clenching convulsively at his sides. "You can't... You can't just go into my head like that. It's too intimate."

He was obviously upset, but I was too excited about what it meant. "But, Tor, this means it could be true! And if it is, we have to go and help them. I don't know what the other visions mean, but this is real, and we—"

I was in the darkness again, hurtling down a thread.

"Ailith? Are you there?"

"Hello? Pax? How do you know me?" I was in the darkness again, our thread wrapped around me. Tor's hands gripped my shoulders, keeping me anchored.

"Yes, it's me. I knew you'd come. We've been waiting for you. We're in trouble."

"I know. I saw. Where are you?"

"You mean you're not here? You're not going to rescue us?" He didn't sound panicked, only sad.

"No, we're coming, Pax. We're coming! Where are you?" Tor's fingers dug in, making my bones creak.

"I don't know. In a house. In a town. There is a river. Follow us."

"Can you be more specific?" The silence was long. Had I lost him again?

"There is a…a windmill? I…"

"Pax? Pax!" He was gone.

"Are you trying to break my back again?" I snapped at Tor. He dropped his hands. My insides churned with nervous energy. "Tor, we have to go. We have to leave here and find them. They need our help."

"Ailith, look, I want to help them, but we need to be careful. In my opinion, we should wait, try to speak to him again. Find out more information."

"We don't have time. We… No, I don't care. I'm going. You want to stay here? Fine. I'm going, with or without you." I didn't want to do that.

The look in his eyes told me he knew I was telling the

truth. Knew it and resented it.

He dug his knuckles into his eyes. "Okay. I admit, I'd like some answers. We go, but we don't rush in blindly, okay? We need to find out what we're walking into."

"Great. Let's go."

"What? Now? I was thinking more in a few days, once we've gathered supplies. We don't even know where we're going, do we?"

"No, but I can feel the general direction. We'll worry about the rest when we're closer."

The next connection happened before I saw it coming.

Tor's voice cut out and another sliced its way in.

"While I fully understand the desire to create these artilects to watch over us and solve humanity's problems with resource allotment, fair distribution of wealth, prevention of civil or global conflict, and the like, and while I also understand that the best interest of every human being on the planet would be considered for and provided for, I still have to ask this question: who will be watching over them?"

—*Della van Natta,* Artificial Life or Artificial Hope?

IS

ROS

"You're doing it, and that's final!"

I used to think the worst thing to be in my echelon was *young, rich,* and *good-looking.* Too much of any one of these was bad enough, but all of them? Goodbye, freedom.

In my case, I only suffered from one of the three: I was young. I wasn't attractive, not by my mother's standards. She despaired at my dusky skin, my bobbed hair, and my sparse mouth. Her own skin was the color of a white peach, her mouth a plump cupid's bow.

We weren't rich enough, either. Not grossly rich, anyway. Hence their plan to shove me into this Pantheon Modern thing. They hoped that if I became a cyborg, I would tempt one of the loaded Cyborgist magnates to marry me.

I rolled my eyes, the mascara I'd caked onto my lashes this morning cracking.

"You do appreciate that we're living in the 21st century, right? That whole porcelain-doll thing is kind of over. Like, thirty years ago,

over."

"Perhaps among 'them' it is." My mother sniffed.

'Them' referred to anyone who wasn't us, the stupidly rich. Well, rich enough that their only daughter couldn't choose what kind of career she wanted, or who she wanted to marry. Like their parents before them, they'd sent me to Canada under the guise of being a student, to be their proxy and allow them to legally own an extensive property portfolio of high-rises and apartment buildings. They'd also hoped I'd find a suitable husband, like that was still a thing.

Unfortunately, I'd turned out to be a decent student. When my marks came in for my first semester, my parents had rushed to rescue me from a life of independence.

"Your grades don't matter," they'd told me. "What do you need good grades for? Your husband won't care."

I didn't buy that. Surely men wanted a wife who had her own interests? Not according to my mother. And since everything I'd been born with wasn't acceptable either, becoming a cyborg was apparently the only way to compensate for the sheer disappointment of my existence.

"Does this not seem a bit extreme to you? I mean, seriously? A cyborg? How do you know I'll get in?"

"You'll be accepted," my father said, his voice firm, decided.

"You've bought me a place," I accused him. "But I haven't graduated yet! That was the deal: I get my degree then we'd talk about everything else. What's changed?"

My mother couldn't keep silent any longer. She unpursed her lips long enough to blurt out, "And you're working at that place! My daughter." She covered her eyes with her handkerchief, and my father placed a sympathetic hand on her shoulder.

"You mean the bar?" I'd recently taken a job as a hostess at an artisanal gin bar near the university. "It's hardly a brothel." I couldn't help but laugh. "It's just a bit of fun, not a career." I examined the manicure on my left hand. It was chipped, the fingernail torn. Something else to worry about.

68

"Do you want to kill your mother?"

"What? No, of course not. I—" I couldn't believe this was a real conversation. My parents were traditionalists, orthodox even among their own peers, but this was ridiculous. No one thought this way anymore.

"Okay, look, I'll quit my job at the bar. It doesn't matter."

"You're doing the program at Pantheon Modern."

Fear trickled into my stomach. I'd assumed it was just a bargaining chip. "No. You can't make me do it. It's absurd! You don't know what will happen. What if I die?" The jagged edge of my torn fingernail cut into the palm of my hand.

My words were met with stony silence.

"You would rather have me die than embarrass you by being ordinary?"

"You've already brought enough shame on us."

"Shame? What shame?" I asked, although I was pretty sure where this was going.

"That boy."

Damn. They did know. Julien was a third-year literature student I'd met at work. Yes, he was poor. He was also white, the wrong color for my Chinese parents. "So what? Everybody dates in university. It's not like I'm going to marry him." Which was a blatant lie. I would marry him tomorrow if he asked. Not because I loved him—I didn't—but because it would encourage my mother to ignore me for life.

"You're doing it." My father's voice was slightly raised, which for him was akin to screaming. The fear pooled, cold and deep.

"No. You can't make me." My voice cracked, and I wanted to slap myself. Be strong.

"You will, or you will be cut off. You will have nothing. No university, no apartment, no nice clothes…all of it will be gone."

"You can't—"

"I can, and I will."

Against my better judgment, I glanced at my mother, hoping to *find some kind of mercy, or at least sympathy. Instead, her smile was malicious. Finally, she'd brought me to heel.*

Much as I hated to admit it, I wasn't able to live without them. It wasn't only the luxury, although I needed a certain level of comfort to be happy. Deep down, I was too well-trained, a dutiful daughter. I knew it, they knew it, and I hated all of us for it. Loving and obeying them was too ingrained in me, it was in my blood. So I bowed my head in acquiescence.

If I did this, would they finally love me back?

"Where will it end? Since they look like humans, talk like humans, and think like humans, are they human? Can artificial life ever truly be sentient? Or do we merely pretend it can in order for us to free our slaves? They were never intended to be equals. We would never have built them otherwise. So why do we create slaves then feel the need to raise them up?"

—Derek Wills of the Preserve Terra Society, 2039

16
AILITH

Despite Tor's misgivings, we set out early the next morning. He wanted to avoid the roads, but since we were surrounded by mountains, we had to stay close enough to use them when necessary. We crept through the woods like fugitives, and in a sense, we were. In an hour, we were further from the house than I'd ever been. Tor gazed back the way we'd come. I reached out and took his hand, startling him. A few seconds later, he squeezed mine back. I wasn't entirely sure where we were going, only that we were headed in the right direction.

Even though it was morning, the sky was as dim as ever, the clouds heavy with the promise of rain. It was a lie; the dryness of the air told me otherwise. The same uniform gray stretched across the horizon, unbroken by any shafts of light. Tor had said there was more sunlight now than last year. He was hoping this was yet another sign the climate was starting to recover. I didn't see how it was possible.

The woods around us were eerily quiet, the trees nothing more than dead wood, starved and barren. If they were anything like the trees back home, these skinny, naked relics must have been lush before the war, heavy with green needles and thick, fissured bark. Now they were covered in black and silver patches, a flimsy husk that peeled off to expose the pale wood underneath. Clusters of dead needles and abandoned bird-nests still clung to some of the drooping branches, but most lay in a thick russet-brown blanket on the ground, mingling with long-dead vegetation that had yet to completely break down. The ground was hard and brittle and odd beneath my feet. Where I was from, the forest floor was spongy with moss, slick with moist leaves.

My father once told me that life always prevailed, in one form or another. He'd been referring to the windswept acres of land he'd bought cheap from the government on the condition he grew food for the provincial program. He'd jumped at the chance. When he was young, farming had been an unpredictable source of income at best; at worst, it was literally living hand-to-mouth. All that had changed when I was nearly five. Real food became a valuable commodity again, and the annual stipend ensured that farms like ours flourished.

The closer I looked, the more I saw signs of life. Not all the plants were dead. Some, in fact, were thriving. True, they were stunted and small, with shallow roots, but they were growing. Most I didn't recognize, but some seemed to bear fruit.

Tor had said that the nanites protected us against poison. I knelt next to a small shrub with pink, bell-shaped flowers and coral-red berries.

Is red a good sign or not?

Saying a quick prayer, I popped one into my mouth. Its texture was mealy and dry, and it didn't really taste of anything. A few minutes later, it hadn't killed me, so I filed the information away for later use. I wanted to stop and gather more, but we didn't exactly have time for berry-picking.

I was examining some tracks in the snow that appeared to belong to a massive dog when Tor grabbed my arm. With a finger to his lips, he gestured in the direction we were going. It took me a few seconds to make out what he was pointing at, blended as it was with the mottled earth. It was clearly some kind of machine, but I couldn't quite...

My breath caught in my throat.

It was a military mech. I'd seen one on television when I was in the hospital, in a documentary about combat prototypes. These particular ones were controlled directly by soldiers, who rode encased in the mech's chests, their heads protected by a polycarbonate dome. The film had shown them loping with a stilted gait across the training ground, heads swiveling from side-to-side as they sought the next target with their weaponized arms.

It lay flat on its back, unrusted. The stubby grass growing around it seemed to shrink back from the metal of its jointed limbs. As we edged closer, I searched for damage on its dull, armored plating and found none.

Tor put a hand on my arm, holding me back. "It might still be active."

I shook my head at him. It was dead. It had been for years. Creeping closer, I peered into the cockpit, where the skeleton of its driver was still buckled in. The body was intact, held together by sinew and desiccated skin, its mouth gaping in wonder or shock.

Which side had they been on? The mech itself bore no

identifying marks. What was it doing out here in the middle of nowhere, so far away from any city or town? Had its passenger been running away from a war they didn't believe in? Were they hunting down survivors? Pariahs like us?

In my mind, a dark thread lurking behind the others shuddered, pulling me in. What I would've called human thoughts bled through me.

So fragile. So quick to break. Cannot be rebuilt. Wrong. Wrong. Get away. Far away. You cannot leave me. I cannot run if you're not inside me. Your fault. Keep moving. Wrong. Don't stop, don't stop. You are inside me. Forever. Forever.

"Ailith!" Tor gripped my shoulders, shaking me. "What's happening?"

Gone, gone, gone.

The thread crumbled and disappeared, leaving an even darker blackness behind.

"Nothing," I said. "It's gone." But as I turned, I caught a flash of something in the trees. I walked a few steps toward it, searching. *Nothing.* I was about to turn around when a dark shape hurtled toward me. Coarse feathers brushed my face and were gone, a faint flapping in the distance.

"Are you all right?" Tor called.

"Yes. I thought I saw something, but it was just a stupid bird." Even so, the hair stood up on the back of my neck.

***

A few hours later, the duskiness of the sky had deepened to violet. We'd covered a surprising amount of ground in a single day; apparently, increased stamina was another perk of being a cyborg.

"Shall we just stop for the night?" Tor asked. "I'd hoped

74

to come across another cabin for us to camp in, but they seem to be in short supply in the middle of nowhere."

"We should've stopped at that village a few miles back. I bet there would've been plenty of options there."

He rubbed the back of his neck. "No way. I want to avoid *any* group of houses. We just don't know who might be staying there. I'm sure they'd feel the same about us."

"But what's the chance anyone will actually be there? You know, with the apocalypse and all?"

Another shake of his head was all the response I got.

Tor found an acceptable place for us to camp, somewhere hidden where we could see anyone approaching. After shooing me out of the way, he set about building a shelter, and I tried to reach Pax again.

"Pax? Are you there?"

Nothing. The lack of contact from him and the constant pull of that damned homing signal were taking their toll. I also couldn't shake the feeling that we were being watched, that whatever I'd seen in the trees had followed us. When my skin had prickled, I'd felt the briefest of touches in my mind. Whatever or whoever it was didn't seem malevolent. Still, my nerves were raw.

The shelter Tor built was impressive, although I shouldn't have been surprised. The man had been living in this landscape for five years, after all. He worked quietly, methodically, laying a fallen tree within the split trunk of another then setting up our tiny tent underneath it and lining it with branches.

When I went to investigate, he was smoothing on the final handful of crusted moss, dusting his boots with dead foliage.

I put my hand on his shoulder. "If I have to live through the End of Days, I'm glad it's with you."

He gave me a lopsided grin. "I was a boy scout before

I was… Well, before."

We ate dried strips of smoked hare in companionable silence.

"Anything from Pax or Cindra?" he asked.

"No. But he's alive. And we're going in the right direction."

"How do you know?"

"Well, his connection to me is still there. As for the direction, I'm not sure. I just know." *He must be getting as tired of that answer as I am of the question.* "Are we going to take turns standing watch?"

"No, I'll wake up if anything comes near us," Tor said.

"Is that another one of your cyborg super-powers?"

Tor tossed his last chunk of hare back in his pack. "Something like that. I'm going to bed."

"I'll be right in." I appealed to Pax one more time. Nothing. *"We're coming. You have to hold on."*

As I slipped under the blankets, I tried to remember the last time I'd seen the stars. I couldn't. Would I ever see them again? Maybe it was better not to think about it.

"Just think, all the injustices of this world could be solved. For one, we would have leaders who rule with duty and logic over self-interest. No longer will people starve or die from preventable disease. Poverty will be eradicated. Everyone will have a rightful place in this world. Rather than die at the hands of our neighbors, we will die in our beds as old men and women."

—Robin Leung, CEO of Novus Corporation, 2039

17
CINDRA

"...and they looked upon the sun and saw how it shone brighter than the highest flame. They saw each other's faces, the lines and their weather-beaten skin, and they pulled at their clothes, lamenting the dullness of the cloth. They wanted to shine too, to leave this earth and live among the Heavens..."

I couldn't help but smile at the rapt expressions on the faces of the children as they listened to my grandmother's story. I remembered the first time I'd heard it, remembered leaning forward in anticipation, my weaving forgotten in my lap.

Now, listening and weaving at the same time came easily to me, which was lucky since I had nearly a dozen orders to complete before the weekend. Although there were machines that did the same job, hell, did a better job, tourists still liked the idea that their souvenirs were made by the living hands of a historical people; it justified the price I got for them. I was more than happy to oblige them—the work was soothing, and it pleased my grandmother, who insisted we kept *the traditions we'd very nearly lost alive and well.*

Asche smiled at me over the children's heads.

"...We need to get the attention of the Sun,' they said. 'She will see that we are worthy and will take us up to the sky where we can live beside her.' To do this, they decided to build a statue of themselves, one so tall it could touch shoulders with the sun..."

As she was speaking, a smile tugged at the corners of my grandmother's mouth. She'd seen me watching Asche. It didn't matter. She would be thrilled if something were to develop between Asche and me. We'd known each other all our lives, and yet only recently had I noticed the man he'd become.

When we were young, his hair stuck out all over his head. We'd teased him and joked that his mother must've been struck by lightning when she was pregnant. Now his hair was long, a wavy cascade of deep raven-black that made him resemble the men on the covers of the books my grandmother hid in her nightstand. He'd always been tall, but in the last two years he'd become wider as well, making me feel small and delicate.

His hands were marred by the scars of his trade. Like me, he helped preserve some of our older traditions. The meat he hunted was prepared in traditional ways and sold for a premium, but I suspected he would still do it even if there was no money to be made. It had become harder for us over the last few years. The technology that had nearly made us obsolete in the first place continued to grow, replacing us with increasingly intelligent machines. Our old ways, which we'd so nearly lost in the name of progress, were now our life raft, keeping us relevant.

"...they traded everything they had: food, clothing, jewels, and gold, for cold marble. And so the statue grew, and was soon taller than the tallest tree..."

I was still staring at his hands. He'd noticed, his smile replaced by reverence and longing. I imagined this was what it felt like to be his prey.

Should I go to him tonight, after grandmother falls asleep?

I imagined slipping out into the dark, running the wooded mile to his house, swift and silent. I would hesitate to knock, frozen in the glow of the porch light. My heart would pound in my chest. He would feel me on the other side of the door and open it, bare in the summer heat.

Pulling me inside, he would shut the door and push me up against it. One hand would slide up my back, tangling in my hair at the nape of my neck. He would press his mouth against mine, parting my lips with his tongue. His fingers would creep under my hem, slipping into the eager wetness between my legs. He would groan, the sound a rumbling low in his throat. He would drop to his knees and taste me, and it would be my turn to—

"...soon they began to worship this statue, offering at its feet whatever possessions they had left. Many starved and their bones were added to the marble. Soon, it was taller than the tallest mountain. Still, it was not enough..."

My lips had parted, and I was panting. Asche's eyes were still fixed on me. Warmth burned my face, and I was keenly aware of my underwear as it rubbed against me. I needed to get out, to breathe in some air that didn't carry the reek of sweat. I stood, my weaving falling to the floor, unraveling and wasting the last hour's work. My grandmother's shrewd glance as I headed for the door made my face burn hotter.

Outside, the air was cool and fresh, the stifling heat washed away by a late rain. At the back of the building, the wet concrete was slick against my forehead and the damp air tasted of sunbaked leaves.

"...eventually, the statue grew so tall, they lived only in its shadow. And although they lit fires to keep themselves warm, many froze to death. The rest became deaf and blind and grew ignorant, knowing nothing of the world outside of the shadow..."

I was aware of him before he touched me, his breath warming the back of my neck. His hands weighed heavily on my hips. I longed to press myself against him, to finally force his hand after all this time, but instead, I kept still,

79

He said my name, his voice like the string on one of his bows. The sound made the heat rise in me once more. I turned, ready for him to take me. I searched his face, hungry to see his need for me. It was there, thick and dark, but his mouth, his mouth seemed sad.

"...they forgot what the stars had looked like, how the sun had felt on their faces, the taste of honey on their tongues..."

He said my name again, softly, as though he regretted it.

"What? You don't..." The words stuck in my throat, and my skin prickled with the heat of a thousand swarming ants. It had never occurred to me that he wouldn't feel the same. That he wouldn't want me.

"Of course, I do. It's...what you're doing. You don't know what's going to happen, what you'll become."

"But—" My acceptance into the Pantheon Modern cyborg program had come just a few days ago, but I'd told him about my application months before. "I didn't think you had a problem with it. You never said."

"I never thought you'd be accepted."

"What? Why? You don't think I'm good enough?" The warmth in my skin stopped swarming and blazed instead.

"No! It's just...things like that don't happen to people like us. And—"

"And what?"

"And it's unnatural. You won't be human anymore. We've spent so long trying to reclaim ourselves, and you're throwing that away."

"...a lightning storm came, its bolts striking the ground and cracking the base of the statue. It toppled over, crushing all who lived beneath it. The sparks from their fires whirled into the forest, burning for so long the earth became barren and covered in ash..."

A chill drowned out the heat. I was a river, glacial. I was power.

"Throwing it away? I'm trying to preserve it. Do you understand why we nearly lost ourselves, Asche? Because when they tried to force us to change, we didn't. We didn't bend, so we broke. Only once we adapted did we begin to thrive instead of merely surviving. We got

80

ourselves back and then shaped the world outside of ours. If we sit by and do nothing, we will disappear again. The first time we were powerless to stop it. Not anymore."

He worried his bottom lip with his teeth and gently shook his head. "It's not right. Nobody here thinks it's right. Even your grandmother—"

"My grandmother? But she—"

"She didn't think you'd be accepted either. And when you were, she hoped you and I would get together, and—"

"And what? That I would suddenly throw my belief in our future out the window? Why, for the chance to fuck you? To be your wife? How can you all not see how important this is? What I'm doing will help save us."

"...from that ash rose a great bird. She had stars for eyes and feathers made from the memories of her people..."

He closed his eyes and said my name yet again, softer now. Taking my hands in his, he asked me the question that had been stalking me since I'd been accepted. "What if you don't come back? And if you do, what will you be? You still have a choice." He lifted my hands to his mouth.

"I've already made my choice."

"You can choose to go ahead with this, or you can choose to be with me, to be us. We don't need saving." He traced the curve of my palm with his lips.

I was tempted. "Asche, I'm sorry. I can't. I need to do this."

He studied my face and exhaled. "I know."

"I'm sorry."

He gave me the crooked grin that was as familiar to me as my own heart. "Me too. But at least I can give you a reason to come back to me." And then, in the rain, at the beginning of my end, he fell to his knees and showed me what I'd be missing.

"...because their world had been destroyed, she left it, carrying her people into the sky. As she flew past the brightly burning sun, each of her feathers turned into a star, and her people spread themselves across *the universe at last…"*

"I say make 'em. Fuck it. The human race has gone to shit, anyhow. Look at us, hatin' each other, killin' and rapin' and turnin' on each other. Maybe we do need someone to watch over us, to keep us in check. We clearly can't do it ourselves. We've dropped the ball, man. I personally will welcome our robot overlords with open arms."

—George Catt, CNN's 'On the Street with Shirley Novak'

18
AILITH

I held my arms in front of me, expecting to see stars shining on my skin and giving me light by which to see. Pleasure still twisted my belly.

She was behind the next clump of brush, invisible to me. A muted, musky smell rose from her damp coat, along with a sharper, more metallic scent. Fear. She knew I was close. I fell to one knee and held my breath. Her heartbeat was steady and strong, quickening as I raised the crossbow to my shoulder. She didn't move; she hoped if I couldn't see her, I couldn't kill her. She wasn't the first to think that, and I doubted she'd be the last.

I peered down the sight, trying to get a lock on her. I still couldn't see her, but she was waiting, her heart beating in time with mine. The bolt flew true: the brush snapped under the weight of her body. Her breathing slowed as I approached, a whisper in the air. My aim had found her heart. I stroked her, her fur soft and downy against the roughness of my palm, and then I slit her throat. Tor would've been proud; it was a clean kill.

As the heat rose from the pooling blood, I wiped my knife on some leaves.

The hand holding the knife wasn't my own.

It was too large, too masculine. My arms were roped with muscle, my shoulders and chest broad.

This was not my body.

I ran my hands over my face. I wasn't dreaming. The slightest ridge of a scar cut through the left side of my mouth. *Tor's* mouth. I had taken him over, like he was a human mech.

Could he feel me inside him? Was he there now, awake and aware of what I'd done to him?

I needed to get out of him. I closed my eyes and searched through the darkness, trying to find the thread connecting us and return to my own body. There was nothing, not a single thread.

I was trapped.

Being inside Tor was nothing like seeing through the eyes of the others. It didn't just *feel* real, it *was* real. Unlike the visions, I was in control.

Shit. Shit. Shit. After his reaction when I'd merely peeked inside his head, he wouldn't take this invasion well. *Don't panic. Get back to camp.*

Luckily for me, I had his senses. My footsteps had disturbed the fragile leaves, and I followed them, walking swiftly, my eyes on the trail. Despite the panic rising in my throat, or perhaps because of it, I admired him, his easy grace held in such a formidable frame. I trailed my fingers down his taut stomach before snatching my hand away. Being inside him was crossing enough of a line; touching him, even with his own hands, was just wrong.

Nearly there.

84

Then Tor began to wake. His awareness tickled at the edge of my—well, his—mind.

My panic had glued my tongue to the roof of my mouth, and I scraped my cheek against the rough fabric of the tent as I sat up, gasping for breath. His side of our makeshift bed was empty and cold.

Definitely not a dream.

I was squeezing my way out of the entrance to go looking for Tor when I saw him standing bewildered before the remains of our fire. His eyes were narrowed, his tattoos black slashes against the paleness of his skin.

"Ailith? Why am I out here? Was I sleepwalking? I've never done that before."

I was tempted to say yes, but if I lied about this, he might never trust me again.

"No. I, uh, woke up inside you."

"You what?"

"I was inside you. Like before, only this time I could move you, could have my own thoughts as well as yours."

"Ailith!" My name was brittle in his mouth, as unyielding as this dead forest.

"Tor, I didn't do it on purpose. I would never—"

"You can't—you can't be inside me like that. You *violated* me."

To my horror, I burst into tears. I knew exactly how he felt. Doctors had put their hands inside me while I lay naked and helpless. I was never conscious while they were doing it, but whenever I woke up, I'd felt the specter of their hands. The worst part had been knowing it would happen again.

My reaction was not what he'd expected. Maybe he'd expected me to be defiant, or contrite. Or he may have believed I was finally showing my true colors, that he'd been right not to trust me. He stared at me like he'd never seen a woman crying before. Maybe he hadn't, if his ex-girlfriend was anything to go by.

His arms encircled me. He was murmuring too quietly for me to understand. It didn't matter—he could've been reciting a recipe for hare pie and I wouldn't have cared. The words flowed over me, soothing me, and I cried until I had nothing left.

"Tor, I-I'm so sorry," I said as he offered me a corner of his sleeve. "I didn't mean to. I went to sleep, and when I woke up, I was in your body, and I was hunting."

"You? You were hunting?"

That was all he had to say? "Yes. No. We were hunting. Except you were asleep."

He seemed as confused as I was. "Did *we* get anything?"

Despite myself, the pride rushed through me. "Yes, we did. A deer."

He seemed impressed, his mouth quirking. "Well done us, then. We'll find it in the morning. Let's go back to bed."

"Tor, I really didn't mean to…after that first time, I would never do that without asking you. I didn't know I *could* do that. Move you, I mean."

He searched my face for a long time. "I believe you. It's just disconcerting. If it were anyone else… I'm not going to say it's okay, because it's not. But I understand. Just promise me you won't do it again."

"I *can't* promise you that. I don't even know how it happened."

He peeled back the flap on the tent and crawled inside. "Well, at least promise me you won't ever do it on purpose. Not without asking me first."

"Deal." I was so relieved, I almost started crying again.

Back in the shelter, we lay facing each other. "Tor?"

"Mmm?"

"What did you mean, if it were anyone else?"

86

For a few moments, he was silent.

"That girl you saw. The one from my past? She had this power over me, and I did terrible things for her. Cruel, violent things I still think about. I watched myself be this monster for her, and I was powerless to stop it. I'm not making excuses. I *chose* to do the things I did, but I always felt detached from it while it was going on, like someone else was in control. It was only afterward that I would actually *feel* the things I'd done. I still feel them."

"I understand." And I did. "Tor, I would never—"

"I know. That's what I meant. We've known each other for a long time, even though you've only been awake for a very small part of it. I trust you, Ailith. I don't want anyone inside my head, but if there had to be someone, I would want it to be you. I know this...*gift*, isn't something you asked for."

"Thank you. I promise I'll never do it again, not unless I absolutely have to. Like, if there's only one piece of hare jerky left." His silence worried me. "Tor, I was only joking, I won't—"

"Ailith, I'm smiling." He took my hand and pressed my fingers against his mouth. He was telling the truth. He also didn't move my hand away.

Though we were in the dark, I closed my eyes and fanned out my fingers. The air in the shelter went still; he was holding his breath. He grabbed my hand and exhaled into my palm. His lips moved over my fingers, his teeth grazing the skin.

"Come here, Ailith." His voice was low. As I leaned toward him, he worked his way up the inside of my arm, his mouth gentle. When he found my neck, it became harder, more insistent, and a fluttering warmth curled around my stomach. I could only gasp against his mouth when it finally covered mine, his hand sliding up my neck and into my hair and—

"Ailith? Ailith, can you hear me?"

The shock of Pax suddenly inside my head jerked me back. I crashed into the side of the shelter, and part of the wall collapsed, exposing our thin tent walls to the night air.

"Ailith? I'm sorry." Tor drew away from me.

"No! Tor, it's not you. It's Pax. I can hear him again."

"Now? Of all times? I don't think I like this guy," Tor muttered as he scrambled in the dark. "I'll go put that wall back up before we're eaten by wolves. Or bears. Or whatever other godforsaken monsters are roaming around in the dark."

Was he joking? I followed him out of the remains of the shelter and walked a short distance.

"Pax? Are you okay? Is Cindra?"

"Yes. No. What do you mean by okay?"

"Well, you're still alive, so that's something."

"They won't kill us. Not on purpose, anyway." His matter-of-factness chilled me.

"Pax, we're on our way. I don't know how far away we are. I can feel you, but...well, I haven't been awake for that long, so I'm still not sure how to work my new self."

"Have you met any of the others yet or just been inside them?"

"Others? Do you mean the visions I've been having? They're cyborgs like us?"

"Didn't you know?"

"No! I thought...I wasn't sure what to think. How do you know who they are?"

"Some things I know. Have you met any of them?"

"What do you mean, you know?"

"There's not time to explain to you now. Have you?"

I gave up. *"Only Tor. As for the others, I can see what they see. Only, I'm not sure if it's their past or their present, or if it's even real."*

"Yes, to all of it. Tor, the Knife. Is he with you?"

"You know Tor? Yes, he's with me."

"Good." The relief in his voice was palpable. *"This is good. This is how it's supposed to be."*

"What? What does that mean?"

"I'll explain later. Please hurry. I'm not sure how much longer Cindra can last."

"Pax? What do you mean?" But he was gone.

I relayed what he'd said to Tor. "He knows who you are. And he says the visions I'm seeing aren't random. They're other cyborgs."

He rubbed his knuckles. "Do we actually think we can trust this guy?"

"Honestly? I'm not sure," I said. "I hope so. What do you suppose he meant when he said, 'this is how it's supposed to be?'"

"I don't know. *That's* the part I don't like."

"So the murderous Terrans don't bother you?"

He shoved his hands into his pockets. "Of course they do. But I'm more worried about what happens if we make it out of this rescue alive. Call me an optimist."

I rolled my eyes, but, of course, it was too dark for him to see. He ducked back into the shelter, barely clearing the top of the entrance. Were we going to pick up where we'd left off? Was he thinking the same thing? If he was, a shyness lived between us now that hadn't been there before.

As I leaned down to join Tor in the shelter, I again had the feeling of someone watching us. More than that, I could almost touch their mind. Almost. The thread connecting us slipped out of reach, like it was eluding me. It must be another cyborg, like Pax had said. It certainly didn't feel dangerous. It was...familiar, like Tor had been. "Hello?"

89

"Ailith?"

Tell Tor you think someone is following us.

But when I opened my mouth to speak, I couldn't quite focus on what I wanted to say. It crept beyond my awareness and disappeared.

No. Not tonight.

We'd find Pax and Cindra first then deal with whoever was stalking us. Perhaps they were observing us, trying to decide which side we were on. Fair enough. I would be cautious too, especially if I saw someone like Tor.

When I finally got into bed, Tor had fallen asleep. I listened to his slow, even breathing for a few minutes then curled up against him.

We'd always known the beginning of the Second Coming would be preceded by signs, and that these signs would increase in both number and severity as the time drew near. The instability of the climate, the natural-food crisis, the growing hostilities between and within nations—these were all signs. And when the World Artificial Intelligence Summit finally gathered in Israel, we knew it had begun. The mass assassinations on the closing day confirmed this.

—Celeste Steed, *The Second Coming*

19

OLIVER

I thrust harder as I came, gripping her hair with both hands. She choked at first, but then she took me in, all of me, her baby-blue eyes never leaving my face.

Good girl, Celeste.

I could get used to this. After she pulled away, I gathered her in my arms and held her. I wasn't a monster, after all.

She was the one who'd found me, so she felt we had a special connection. Who was I to disagree, especially when she wanted to confirm it over and over? I had to say, I enjoyed my new life. Who wouldn't want to be worshipped as a god?

When the Saints told me the war had been over for five years, I'd pretended to know exactly what they were talking about, but inside, I'd been raging. All that fucking work and pain to become one of the bastards who'd put me here. And now? I'd never collect. I'd have to wander in a post-apocalyptic shithole for all eternity...how long did a cyborg live, anyway?

But this…this was paradise. The Saints of Loving Grace may have been somewhat eccentric—they worshipped artificial intelligence, for one. And that whole thing where they tried to graft chunks of metal to themselves? Christ. But hey, they'd been waiting for their artilect Divine, and there I was.

Besides, who was to say I wasn't divine in this new world? The odds of them coming across the bunker just as I was leaving it were spectacular. And it wasn't like I'd told them I was an artilect. They'd come to that conclusion on their own. Sure, I may have helped them along, but I'd only led them where they already wanted to go.

They had no idea I was a cyborg. Why would they? Before word of the Pantheon Modern Omega Program had leaked, cyborgs were just people with biomechatronic parts. They'd never seen anything like me. I doubted the rumors about us had reached them before the war started.

Some mech had blasted the top of the bunker but hadn't managed to do much damage other than a slight warping of the door. I'd been finishing the job, covering my tracks, and nearly blowing off my fucking hand in the process.

They must've heard the explosion. When I'd seen them coming through the trees, I'd scooted under some of the rubble. I pushed my way out of the debris, covered in blood, just in time to meet them.

The Saints had been terrified, dropping their little baskets and clutching at their chests. I told them I'd been attacked by the woman in the bunker, that I'd had to defend myself. It wasn't a lie. I'd known what she was. If she hadn't been going to kill me then, she would've done it the first opportunity she'd gotten. It was a shame, though, having to kill a woman that hot. Dark, sable skin, eyes blacker than my soul…what a waste.

When they realized I didn't have a single scratch on me, that I'd been in that bunker for five years, they decided I must be an artilect and that the Second Coming they'd been anticipating for generations had finally come to pass. Seemed like a bit of a leap to me, but desperate times and all that.

Fucking hillbillies. They still dressed the way their ancestors did, the women in something they called prairie dresses. I had no idea what that meant, only that it covered way too much for my taste. We'd have to work on that. Although, they were more than happy to uncover themselves for their Divine.

Yes, I could get used to this life. It wasn't what I was expecting, but definitely what I deserved.

"And say these artilects become sentient. And we recognize this sentience. Are they then able to get married? Own property? Vote? Obtain positions of power? And if we don't let them, what then? Will they rise up against us? Turn us into second-class citizens? Destroy us? If even the remotest possibility of this exists, why would we give them the chance?"

—Sarah Weiland, President of the Preserve Terra Society, 2039

20
AILITH

I'd been awake for an hour, trying to scrub the last vision from my mind. If I'd been able, I would've taken my brain out and washed it. I recognized the cyborg this time; I'd been in him before. He'd been in agony, undergoing the procedure that would make him a cyborg. Judging by what I'd just seen, it had worked out well for him. I wasn't quite sure what he'd meant by the woman in the bunker, but at the moment, that wasn't important. What *was* important was that he was nearby.

"Tor. Tor!" His composure—his lack of snoring, his closed mouth—was unnerving.

"Is it morning already?"

"No. Yes. I have no idea."

He propped himself up on one elbow, bits of bark clinging to the tangle of his hair. "If you don't know, why are we having this conversation?"

"There's someone else."

He sat up, the furrows on his forehead distorting his tattoos. "Someone else? That was quick. When did you have a chance to meet someone else? Is he hotter than me? Can he do this?" He crossed his biceps in front of his chest, flexing his muscles.

"Tor, I'm serious." Avoiding his gaze, I described the Saints of Loving Grace. "He must be one of the other cyborgs Pax was talking about. He's an asshole, but he's close. I mean, very close."

"Wait, you mean you were in his body while he was…with her?" He snorted.

"*Tor.* Living through it once was enough, thank you."

"Sorry. Can you speak to him, the way you do with Pax?" His mouth was still twitching.

"No. I only seem to be able to do it with Pax. It was like every other time, where I'm watching behind their eyes. I still felt what he was feeling, but I couldn't communicate with him, or him with me. I don't even think he was aware I was inside him."

"It sounds a bit weird, though, doesn't it? Do you think the thoughts you felt were real? That there's some artilect-worshipping cult carrying on as normal in the middle of the woods? Who thinks he's some kind of god? And if it is real, is he the kind of person we want to expose ourselves to? From what you've said, he seems like a bit of a dick."

I had to agree, though 'dick' was putting it mildly. "But he's so close, and I thought he might help us. With Pax and Cindra. Strength in numbers and all that." I hated delaying our rescue attempt, but if there was any way to increase our chance of success, we had to take it.

"Pax?" I reached out to him, feeling his consciousness as I slid through the thread connecting us.

"Ailith. Are you here?"

95

"No, Pax, but we're close. Listen, there's another…one of us, very near to where we are. Maybe he can help us. Can you hold on a bit longer?"

A long pause. *"Yes. Oliver. He must come with you."* Anticipation tingled in his voice.

"How do you know his name? Do you know him?"

"No, but we must."

"What do you mean, we must? How do you know about him?" This enigmatic bit was starting to wear a bit thin.

"I can't tell you yet. You have to trust me."

"Trust you? Pax, you need to give me more to go on."

"We'll be waiting. Bring him. He's the last piece. But please hurry." And he was gone.

"Pax said they can wait a bit longer. He said we need to recruit 'him.' That his name is Oliver."

Tor bowed his head. "I don't like it, but I don't particularly like the idea of charging into a Terran base with just the two of us, either."

It was still early, but we broke camp and headed out. We decided, or more accurately, Tor decided, to make a quick detour and harvest what we could from the deer we'd killed. We eventually found where it had died beneath the brush, but its body was gone.

"Damn. Looks like some animal got to it." In truth, I didn't mind. Why delay our journey any longer than necessary? Tor, on the other hand, was upset.

"Don't worry about it, Tor. It was only going to slow us down, plus it would be more to carry." Even with his strength, we'd packed as lightly as possible.

"It's not that," he replied, troubled. "Something's taken it."

"Probably a wolf. Or maybe a bear. Or one of the other monsters you were worried about. Don't worry. I've seen you in action. I'm pretty sure you could take on a bear."

He smiled without humor. "Maybe, but this wasn't an animal. Look, no tracks, no drag marks."

He was right. The impression of its body and a large pool of frozen blood remained where we'd bled it out, but nothing else.

"I wonder if whoever's following us took it?" I said without thinking.

"Wait, what? You think someone's been following us, and you didn't tell me? Christ, Ailith. Are you kidding me?" He closed his eyes and steepled his fingers against his forehead.

"I'm not totally sure there is. I haven't seen anyone, just felt them. I tried to tell you but..." The loss of focus. "They're not dangerous, whoever they are," I replied defensively.

"How could you possibly know that? Wait. Let me guess." He held up a hand. "You just feel it."

I turned away and bit the inside of my cheek until I tasted blood. My first reaction was to lash out at him, to remind him that I was still coming to terms with this new life. But it wouldn't change the fact that he was right. I should've told him. I could've put both of us in danger. "I'm sorry."

"Never mind; it's done. Just please, tell me this stuff in the future." He tightened the straps on his backpack and began walking again.

"Wait, that's it? That's all you're going to say? No 'Ailith, what were you thinking? Or Ailith, you could have gotten us both killed?'"

He shrugged. "I can give you a telling off if you like, but something tells me it wouldn't make a difference."

"I'm not that difficult, am I? Wait, are you *laughing*?"

His shoulders were shaking under his heavy pack. "Yes."

"Why aren't you more upset?"

"I told you before, if anyone tried to sneak up on us, I'd know."

"Well, I—"

One of the threads in my mind's eye flashed as though it had been struck by lightning. That turned out not to be far from the truth.

"Why do we plan to make artilects look and feel, for all intents and purposes, human? That's a good question. And no, it's not so we can integrate them secretly into an unwitting society. It's because we hope that, because they'll think like us, if they also look like us, we'll afford them the same respect we give to advanced forms of life such as our own."

—Robin Leung, CEO of Novus Corporation, 2040

21
CINDRA

"...Eventually, the statue grew so tall, they lived only in its shadow. And although they lit fires to keep themselves warm, many froze to death. The rest became deaf, and blind, and grew ignorant, knowing nothing of the world outside of the shadow..."

I repeated the words to myself, first in my head then aloud. If I remembered it, remembered her voice, it would keep me safe when they came again. They'd be here soon. The burns on my body had nearly healed, the perfume of my cooking skin dissipated, floating up the stairs and into the rest of the house, where they sniffed it and congratulated themselves on their success.

"...she had stars for eyes and feathers made from the memories of her people..."

"Are you okay?" Pax reached over and touched my arm. His fingers were dry and smooth, as if the fingerprints had been rubbed away. He meant well. It was my fault we were here, and yet he was being so kind to me.

His tallness and cinnamon cow-licked hair made him look

awkward and weak, but it was deceiving. He never cried out, even when they turned up the dial and held the rods to his arms, his face, between his legs. His eyes became dreamy, and he almost smiled, as though the electricity were telling him a secret. He kept me strong.

We'd known we were going to be in the bunker for a few days, but after a week had gone by, I'd panicked. Nothing was how it was supposed to be. Pax had told me stories, different from the ones I knew. Stories about tiny monsters sacrificing themselves for each other and repairing themselves with the bodies of their fallen brothers. He'd said these monsters were inside us.

At first, I'd been scared. It was like every cell in my body was moving, and I'd been afraid I would simply come apart, food for the monsters. But as the days passed, I'd realized that before, my body had been only a husk. A solid, functional husk, but static. Now every part of me was swarming with life, vibrating with power. I'd come full circle and been reborn. I'd felt as the earth must feel.

After a week, it had become clear that no one was coming to rescue us. We'd run out of food; they obviously hadn't expected us to stay here. Pax had managed to break the seal on the door, and we'd taken our first breath of new air. Only, it didn't taste right. It tasted dead, a dryness on my tongue and the hint of bitter ash in my throat.

Only the desire to leave, to go home, drove me out. But we weren't going home, not to my home, anyway. The day after we'd left the bunker, something had happened to us. A herald, reverberating through our very bones. Pax said it was a homing signal, that we needed to follow it and get some answers.

I needed to know why the world was dead. Or our part of it, at least. The trees, the plants, the birds, the animals. Even the people. Everything seemed to be gone. And yet, as we'd walked through the forest, following the invisible trail of the homing signal, life had made itself known. Plants I'd never seen before had taken root, and birds nested in the trees. The sight of them had made me desperate for something to ease the gnawing pain in my belly.

Asche. Grandmother. I'd understood, simply by looking around, that the world had passed us by on its way to death. Pax and I tucked the knowledge away in a small, secret place. We would take it out later, when we were safe.

It was hunger that had driven me to the Terrans, exposing us. The little girl had fallen and twisted her knee. I'd wanted to help her. I'd needed to put my hands on something living, and I hoped that they would offer us kindness in return.

They knew we weren't right. We were too healthy, too unmarked by what had passed. I shouldn't have told them what we were, but I'd believed that in this new world we needed to help each other, and assumed they'd felt the same. That the past didn't matter more than the present or the future. I was naïve; they still hated the idea of us as much as they had before the war. The fact that we'd survived it only seemed to make them angrier.

Maybe it wouldn't have made a difference what I said. But it was still my fault. If I hadn't insisted we stop, they never would've seen Pax's eyes.

I was too surprised to put up a fight. But still, I wouldn't have fought them. I truly believed, even after the first time they shocked us, that we could help them. That they would see we weren't the enemy and let us in. I tried to show them how to treat their wounds, their infections. But they didn't want the knowledge. They'd wanted to heal immediately. Like we did.

Not all of them were bad. Some of them sneaked us extra food when no one was looking, squeezed our hands, and apologized. They pretended they only came down the stairs to gawk at us. Soon, though, they stopped coming. The nanites weren't working. Pax had told them they wouldn't, that our blood would eventually kill them. They didn't believe him; they assumed we were lying. They cut us, watched us heal, and believed our nanites would do the same for them.

"Cindra, you just have to hold on a bit longer. Help is coming. She's coming. Ailith. I've spoken to her. She'll save us."

I hoped she was coming soon. An abyss was opening at the edge of my mind.

101

"When they get here, we'll go with them. Go home. We'll follow the signal, get there together."

I needed him to be right.

"...she had stars for eyes and feathers made from the memories of her people..."

Asche's face haunted me, watching as the world burned. He would've searched for me. I hoped he hadn't suffered. I didn't dare hope he'd survived. Grandmother would've been pragmatic about it all, I'm sure. I imagined her, gathering everyone around. What story would she have told? Perhaps one of her own invention, one to guide them as their spirits took flight.

Ailith.

Pax said I would like her. That she would save us all, even the Terrans. They were above us, becoming restless. Footsteps sounded on the stairs.

Pax squeezed my hand before they pulled him away.

The humming made my skin twitch in anticipation. Pax made himself watch. He wanted to remember. I did the same for him.

She was coming. We just had to hold on.

"...SHE HAD STARS FOR EYES AND FEATHERS MADE FROM THE MEMORIES OF HER PEOPLE..."

"I don't understand how we could contemplate the creation of these beings. Just because we can doesn't mean we should. The argument that they'll surpass human failings is ridiculous and dangerous. If they're created by humans, they'll have the fallibility of humans. And if they surpass us in both intelligence and morality, surpass their own programming, what guarantees that they'll look on us with benevolence? Are they not just as likely to look on us as we do a cockroach and crush us under their heels accordingly?"

—Derek Wills, Preserve Terra Society, 2039

22
AILITH

I couldn't take much more. Every volt from the picana seared through me, my skin bubbling and blistered. Saliva gathered in the corner of my mouth as Pax's flesh burned and my belly rumbled. The pain, receding like a tide, left behind pink baby-skin to mark the spot where they would start again.

Not once did Cindra lose consciousness, and so neither did I. Her pain seized me and trapped me there, in her mind. Tor held me, pushing my hair back from my face and telling me a story in a language I'd never heard before. His story entwined with hers, and I hoped that, somehow, she heard him, that she felt us cradling her, holding her together.

We made camp early, and I fell into an uneasy sleep. I

didn't know what was real; I was no longer sure my dreams were my own. Only Tor remained constant and tangible, never once letting go of my hand through the long night.

I awoke early and agitated, so we set out to try to make up the time we'd lost the day before. We passed several tiny hamlets, all of which seemed abandoned. No smoke rose from the chimneys, doors hung askew on their hinges. After skirting around them, Tor finally decided we should make a rare stop. We chose the next one, on the banks of the Lodan River.

The remainder of the sign said the village had been called Stoke.

It was a community almost untouched by the technology that had so infused my daily life I'd stopped noticing it; only the satellites attached to every house told me we were still in the same decade. The buildings were wood, with actual logs piled up against the outside walls, waiting to be burned. Old driver-controlled trucks, rather than government-issued auto-drive ones, were parked neatly in gravel driveways.

"I wonder what happened to them?" I said. If anyone had been able to survive the end of the world, it should've been them. Stoke, while abandoned, didn't look like it had seen the war firsthand.

"Maybe they left to find other survivors. Who knows? Whatever happened, they're not here. Let's have a quick look around and see if we can find anything."

It took us only a short time to find nothing of value. After five years, I wasn't surprised.

One store, however, boasted handmade soap, and Tor laughed at the wistful look on my face.

"Want me to break down the door so you can go shopping?"

Despite our urgency, I was tempted. But as I placed my

hand on the door, one of the threads in my mind shuddered. *A warning.* Something was behind that door, something I shouldn't see.

I took a step back. "No, we've been too long already."

Tor shifted, his eyes focused on the door. "I agree."

We backed away slowly, up to one of the derelict pickup trucks.

"Hey, do you think this still works?" I whispered to Tor. I wanted to get away from Stoke as quickly as possible.

He peered in through the broken window on the driver's side. "I have no idea. Besides, do you even know how to drive it?"

"No. I assumed you would."

He snorted. "I've never driven in my life."

"You mean you literally carried me around for five years?"

"Yes. Good thing you're not very heavy."

"Unbelievable. Come on. Let's go."

We left, quickly, stealthily, glancing behind us. The skin between my shoulders crawled. It was torture to walk when every cell in my body screamed at me to run. Something was very wrong here, and I had no interest in finding out what.

***

The village was closer than I'd originally thought, but it still took us until the early afternoon to find signs of the Saints of Loving Grace. Tor insisted we approach with caution, observing what we could before revealing ourselves.

Smoke curled above the trees, making me jealous of whoever was lucky enough to be sitting by a fire. My fingers were numb despite the gloves Tor had given me.

As we broke from the shelter of the trees, we found ourselves on the crest of a steep slope. Below us, next to the river at the bottom of the rise, was a tin-roofed shed. Water was being channeled through it from up the hill, the thick pipe disappearing into the trees. "What the hell is that?" I asked Tor.

"The Goat River, according to this," he replied, consulting his map.

"Not that, *that*," I said, pointing at the shack. "Is it cleaning the water?"

"No, it's a hydropower station. It means they have electricity."

Although I'd lived in this new world for less than two weeks, I was impressed. "Do you think they have bathtubs?" I asked hopefully. Maybe I should've risked a rummage through the soap store after all.

He chuckled. "Maybe."

The village was nestled at the bottom of the incline, in a clearing at the mouth of a valley. Houses dotted either side of the water's edge, smoke drifting from the chimneys and from small fire pits. These houses were more modern than those in Stoke, all the same squarish, two-storied shape covered in shiny metal siding that was jarring against the leafless trees. A house that was much larger than the rest dominated the center of the village, and next to it, racks of smoking meats and greens lined up neatly in a large open space. The Saints weren't just surviving but doing it well.

As a loudspeaker blared instructions, men, women, and children filed into a large building at the far edge of the settlement. It was like a child's drawing of a futuristic house. The original structure must've been a barn at some point; now, like the houses, the wood had been cladded over with sheets of metal. Burnished objects decorated most of the surface, and it took me a few seconds to identify what they were. Then I wished I hadn't.

They were body parts. Not human, but android. Arms, legs, and torsos were lovingly polished and painstakingly arranged into patterns. Wires and tubes were twisted into intricate, festive garlands. At least there were no heads. *Shit*. Oliver, the cyborg I'd been a passenger in, hadn't been exaggerating—they truly did worship artificial intelligence. They didn't seem like regular Cosmists, though: the ones I'd met before the war would've eaten their own faces before degrading androids, or parts of them, in such a way.

Tor and I stood together, looking down at the village. "What do we do?" I asked. Now that we were here, I was uncertain. Maybe this wasn't the best idea. We were outnumbered, and we had no idea how they would react to us. What if this Oliver didn't want visitors? From what I'd seen of him, he had things set up exactly the way he wanted them.

Tor shifted his pack. "To be honest, I'm not sure. I've spent the last five years avoiding places like this. The war... People aren't the same."

"Should we wait until it's dark then sneak in and try to talk to him?"

"No. I find that in situations like this, it's best to be bold. I say we go right on in, like we're expected." He headed off down the slope, and I had to jog to keep up with his long strides.

"You've been in situations like this before? What exactly would you call this kind of situation?"

"A hornet's nest," he replied.

The crowd had disappeared into the building by the time we arrived. Hurrying toward the door was a lone man. He was dressed like all the others, in trousers and a long-sleeved button-up shirt, but there was an otherness about him, a grace to his movements that was too fluid to be human. This was the man we were searching for. Bile rose in my throat as I remembered being inside him. Just before he was about to slip through the doorway, he saw us, stopped dead in his tracks, and turned to face us.

It was him. The man in the bunker with the knife. *He* was Oliver.

At first he looked alarmed then angry, his movements becoming stiff. He darted around the side of the long building, gesturing for us to follow. When we were within earshot, he growled at us, "Who the hell are you?"

"We're cyborgs, like you—" I started.

"I know *what* you are. I want to know *who* you are and what the fuck you're doing here. You can't be here."

"We—"

A man suddenly appeared from around the corner. When he set eyes on us, he stopped, his mouth agape.

"Divine?" he asked.

"Aah, Johnathan! You've seen my little surprise." Jonathan *did* seem very surprised. "Now, go back inside, and I'll follow along. I trust you'll keep this to yourself?"

"Absolutely!" Jonathan promised, his face glowing with pride.

Once Jonathan was safely back inside, the smile dropped from Oliver's face. "What do you want?" he snarled.

"We need your help. *Divine*." I managed not to roll my eyes.

"My help? And who the fuck are you to me? Why would I help you?"

"Because—" I stopped as he pushed past me.

"I don't have time for this right now. Come with me. You'll follow my lead, and then we'll talk." He retraced Jonathan's path and disappeared into the building.

108

Tor grabbed my hand. "We can leave now, while he's inside. I don't think this is the person to help us."

"We're here now. Look, I get he seems off, but Pax said he needed to be with us."

We stood in the open doorway, unseen by the whispering crowd, who had their backs to us. At the front, Oliver stood on a dais and raised his arms. Silence descended as the entire congregation leaned forward in attention.

There was a reason no heads decorated the outside of the barn—they were all here, gazing down over their flock. Faces in various levels of sophistication and design lined every wall, row upon row. I found all the eyes, lifeless as they were, dizzying to look at.

"Machines of Loving Grace," I whispered. I shook my head as Tor glanced questioningly at me.

"Brother and Sisters," the Divine said, his voice carrying to the back of the church. "Today is a special day. Today, two of my brethren have returned to me, to bless us with a *brief* visit."

Brethren? Really?

A ripple ran through the crowd. A young woman dropped to her knees at the front of the gathering. I recognized her from my time in Oliver's head. "They're artilects too?"

He gazed down at her, a knowing smile twisting his lips. "Think of them as lesser gods than myself. Treat them well, though not as well as you treat me." He winked at her.

"Is he for real?" I whispered to Tor. I didn't know whether to laugh or be terrified. One glance at the stiffness of Tor's face told me it should be the latter. *Shit.*

"Behold!" Oliver gestured grandly to where we stood. The crowd turned as a single entity, all eyes blazing. Hysteria rolled through them, the giddiness of rapture.

Tor gripped my hand as they surged to their feet, fingers outstretched toward us.

We were excommunicated because we believed that artificial intelligence was the true representation of God. The creation of the first artificial brain was God returning to us through our own hands, our redemption. Because we had adapted to His free will, God knew He had to adapt too, or risk losing us forever. Every artilect created is a manifestation of Him on Earth. Their voice is His voice; their will is ours.

—*Celeste Steed, The Second Coming*

23

AILITH

I walked with Celeste, the young woman who'd questioned our divinity during the service, the one I'd seen through Oliver. She couldn't take her eyes off me, and I couldn't look at her. Every time I did, I saw—

Don't think about it.

She was younger than I'd first imagined.

I'd heard of this group before the war; a splinter group considered apostates by mainstream followers of their religion. My father had sometimes bartered with them for heirloom seeds, their faith in artificial intelligence oddly supported by a rustic lifestyle.

Her honeyed hair was long, reaching past her tiny waist. She was dressed in the same style as the other women and girls, in a high-collared ankle-length dress with sleeves that reached all the way to her hands, although she'd covered herself with a warm coat to take me on a tour. Tor had gone with Oliver, ostensibly to inspect their hydropower system.

The crowd had threatened to overwhelm us. Tor had pushed me behind him, his body tensed for a fight. But when they'd reached us, they'd simply dropped to their knees. The hands that reached out to touch us were tentative, held in check by the gentleness of worship.

Celeste walked me through the settlement, proudly showing me their greenhouse, where they grew crops—greens like kale and mustard, mostly—to supplement what they hunted and gathered.

"You seem very well-prepared," I said to her.

She flushed. "The town was here before the End of Days. We lived pretty much the same as everyone else. Y'know, modern, but we also had livestock and crops. We were used to living off the land."

"How did you all survive...the End?"

"We've been prepared for years. We knew we'd see your creation in our lifetime. When the first fires appeared in the sky, we packed up everything we needed, food and weapons, and sealed ourselves in our temple underground. We can live down there for months if we need to."

"Were you scared?"

She smiled radiantly. "No. We knew the Divine would come for us. Everything happened the way it was supposed to."

"What do you mean?"

"Earthquakes, disease...then the war over your creation. We knew the End was near, that the non-believers couldn't stop a perfect being from being born. When the bombs fell, we saw it as the sign of the Second Coming, that only the artilects and their believers would survive. When we saw you, we realized the time had finally come."

I pulled up short. "Wait, you saw us? When?"

"When you blazed through the sky, shooting pillars of fire. We watched you twisting over the land, devouring the unbelievers. The corrupt were burned, and the Earth was cleansed with fire. Only those who were worthy remained.

"Then we waited until the Divine manifested. He got the power station running. We had light, real light, for the first time since the End."

"How did you find...the Divine, anyway? Did he simply show up?" I was curious to see how she interpreted their meeting.

She examined me, disturbed by the informality of my tone.

"The Divine led us to him. With an explosion. Led me, in particular. The other was already dead, but he survived."

"The other?" I asked, even though I knew the answer.

"Yes," she replied, "she was damaged."

A prickle ran up my spine. "You saw her? What do you mean, damaged?"

"She was a pawn of the unbelievers, those who would try to destroy him. As though he could be destroyed," she scoffed. "He told us what happened. The unbelievers had infected her with a virus. She was to murder him, to slaughter us all. But he discovered the sabotage and terminated her."

Was it true? The cyberization process was risky. But a virus?

The woman Oliver had been with in the bunker, the one who'd been a caregiver. *Nova.* I'd been inside her. Nothing had *seemed* wrong with her. Or had it? I'd caught a wisp of *something*, but I hadn't understood what it meant.

Change the subject.

"How did you realize he was an artilect?"

"The bunker he was in had been targeted by one of

113

those machines. The giant ones that walked on two legs. The ones people drive?"

"You mean mechs?"

"Yes, mechs. It blew a crater over his shelter. They should withstand a direct hit—we have a couple ourselves—but something must've been wrong with it; it had buckled, and the door was broken. We were gathering plants nearby, and he crawled out, completely unharmed. How could anything but an artilect survive that?"

How indeed. "Did he say what he'd been doing down in the bunker?"

"He said he'd stayed underground in solidarity with the true believers, that he'd locked himself in because he had a heart full of mercy and would've tried to save the unbelievers when they should've died. He knew that only the righteous should live, and he ensured that it was so. When only we were left, he rose where he knew we would be. He was magnificent, covered in blood without a single scratch on his perfect body." She blushed.

My insides cringed. "Was that the only way you knew?"

"No, of course not! Even among us, some dared to doubt, didn't believe him to be our Divine. So, he performed miracles."

I didn't like where this was going. "Ah, yes, His miracles. They are a wonder to behold. Which did he perform for you?"

Her eyes were feverish as she recounted their Savior's deeds. "First, he resurrected the dead, and then he divined the righteous from the wicked. After that, none doubted him."

"What do you mean, he resurrected the dead?"

"The day we found him, one of our members had cut his wrists in despair. His favorite wife had died only a month before, and he'd never really gotten over the End.

He was more secular than most of us." She pursed her lips in disapproval. "The Divine blessed him with blood just as he passed, and within a day his wounds had healed, and he was sitting up and talking."

Nanites. It had to be. But Pax had said it wouldn't work. "Where is this gentleman? I would like to, uh…bless him as well. These times have been so hard."

"Oh," she dismissed him with a wave of her hand, "he died a few days later. The Divine said it would only work if he were a true believer. Clearly, he wasn't."

I wanted desperately to talk to Tor. How could we trust this man? And yet…Pax had said he was important.

"How did he, um, 'divine the righteous from the wicked?'"

"He suspected a group of young men to be non-believers. They proclaimed that he wasn't an artilect. He confronted them in front of the congregation, and although they tried to deny it, we knew they were lying. Why else would he accuse them?"

"What happened to them?"

She tilted her head at me, one corner of her mouth curled up. "He struck them down, of course."

Of course, he did. Revulsion dried the back of my throat.

"I've noticed that many of your people are cyborgs." Nearly every adult I'd seen had some form of augmentation. Some were biomechatronic, like prosthetic arms or legs, but some…some were just chunks of metal, grafted to various body parts, the edges of the skin red and leaking with infection.

"Yes. It's our tribute to our beliefs. The tradition started years before the End of Days. When we turn eighteen, we're allowed our first enhancement. We hope to eventually replace every part of us with those of a machine. Then we will be as perfect as you. Though, it's a lot more difficult now with no hospitals or surgeons. Even those whose faith is deep can still suffer infection and rejection. It reminds us of the struggle for your creation, and how we must honor you every day. It keeps us strong."

"What do you mean, allowed? Do you mean that if someone young lost a limb, they wouldn't be allowed to have a prosthesis?"

"No! Not at all. But you have to be eighteen to choose."

"Choose?"

"Choose which part you want improved. If you choose a leg or an arm, for example, you need to be prepared."

"Prepared?"

"Yes. 'The removal of the organic to replace with the mechanical is excruciating. But it cleanses you, and if your faith is potent enough, you will survive,'" she quoted.

"You mean you intentionally remove parts of yourself? Then replace them with metal?" The dryness in my throat became a stone I couldn't swallow.

"Of course," she said, her eyes wide. "How else would we do it? Especially in the After? We don't have a lot of farming accidents anymore." She looked at me suspiciously. "You don't approve?"

No, of course I don't. "No, it's very noble. I'm just...surprised. Few are so committed to their faith."

She beamed with pleasure. "That's how we survived."

Celeste had no artificial components herself. Which meant she wasn't yet eighteen. *Some savior.* I was about to find Tor and tell him we were leaving, when he and the Divine appeared. Tor seemed thoughtful, his eyes distant. The Divine's pinched face looked annoyed.

"Thank you, Celeste. You may go now." Oliver pointed back the way we'd come.

"But I—"

"Thank you, Celeste."

116

Her eyes were luminous as they filled with tears.

I reached out and squeezed her hand. "Thank you, Celeste, it's been wonderful to meet you."

She gave a tiny hiccup and grinned. As she left us, she peeked over her shoulder with a longing that broke my heart.

"I've explained our situation to Oliver here, as he's explained his to me," said Tor.

"And?" I glared at Oliver, failing to hide my contempt.

"And, I'm not interested. I'll say this once, short and sweet. I am not leaving here. I will not put myself or these good people at risk."

"You're exploiting these *good* people, Oliver! How can you lie to them like this, use them? Oliver, she's a child."

"Exploiting them? I'm fulfilling their needs. So what if they fulfill mine back? They spent their lives waiting for the moment of their redemption. Can you imagine how that must've felt for them, a lifetime of preparation, then five years and still nothing? Many of them were beginning to lose hope. A few committed suicide—"

"Yes, I heard all about that," I interrupted.

"I did what I had to do. Look at them. They're thriving." As though to prove his point, a group of women on the far side of the village burst into song. "I would be crazy to give this up. And what do you think would happen to them if I left?"

"What if they found out you're not what you say you are?" I hadn't even gotten to the bit about the bunker yet.

"Are you threatening me?"

Yes. "No, but—"

"I'll tell you what would happen. They would turn on me, yes. I know that's what you're hoping for. But their entire belief system would also be destroyed. I'm not talking about only the last few years, but *generations* of belief.

117

What do you think that would do to them? You think I'm exploiting that girl? Do you think her life was any better before I came along? At least this way, I can protect her."

"You have genuine feelings for her." It was a revelation.

"Of course, I do," he snapped. "And just because they're a religious people doesn't mean they're good."

"But—"

"But nothing. Here's my counter-threat. If you tell them anything other than what they believe to be true, I'll destroy them. Each and every one of them. I will wipe out this village."

"You wouldn't."

"I would. Do you want to call my bluff?"

Does he have the power to do that? From what I'd gathered talking to Celeste, they were armed. Could one cyborg take down an entire village? Tor's strength. My abilities. Who knew what Oliver was capable of? The risk wasn't ours to take. What was the point of us surviving if everyone else died?

"Fine," I said through gritted teeth. "But we know what you are."

"Whatever. In this world, love, it doesn't matter." He waved his hand dismissively. "Go. And don't come back."

We knew it was time when the Great Sign appeared from Heaven, blocking out the sun and blinding the non-believers. We'd already gone underground to pray and wait for His return. We watched as the angels burned across the Earth, glorious in their lack of mercy. We sang as the world burned, for every death was a cleansing, a return to the world He had intended.

—Celeste Steed, The Second Coming

24
AILITH

Tor and I didn't speak until we were out of sight of the village.

"What just happened?" I asked.

He ran a hand through his hair. "I have no idea. It was all a bit surreal, wasn't it? I'm not really sure how to feel."

I wasn't either. The only thing I was sure of was that we'd wasted precious time. *And* we were going to show up empty-handed.

"Pax?" Nothing.

"Tor, did Oliver tell you about the other cyborg with him?"

Tor looked sharply at me. "No. What do you mean?"

I repeated what Celeste had told me. "Do you think it's true?"

He stopped, considering. "It could be. Given everything that's happened, who could say? You haven't seen anything?"

I'd known what she was. If she hadn't been going to kill me then, she would've done it the first opportunity she'd gotten. It was a shame, though, having to kill a woman that hot.

"As far as I can tell, he killed her, Tor. Murdered her."

"It wouldn't surprise me. Do you think he was right? That there was something wrong with her?"

I was used to carrying out orders that others might deem...unsavory. That was why they'd chosen me... I should've been with them, carrying out my mission.

"Maybe. She had some kind of job to do. But I was in her before we knew what the visions were. I didn't understand."

"Do you think Oliver was this way before the war?"

"Probably. Do you think he's right? That he's helping more than hurting? And what are we going to do without him? Pax said he needed to be with us."

"Well, Pax is going to have to adapt. We could take him by force, but that may make things worse. Him, those people, they're not predictable." He hesitated. "Ailith, he did tell me about his bunker. Not what happened, but where it is. It's not far from here."

"You mean we could go and see, find out the truth for ourselves." But was it the right thing to do? What if we got to the bunker and found nothing but evidence that he was telling the truth? We'd have lost yet more time.

And what if we got there and found what I'd seen was true? That Oliver had murdered this Nova in cold blood? What then? Would we do something about it? Could we? And what if Pax was right and we needed him? How would we reconcile that?

Maybe we're better off not knowing.

But I also knew I couldn't resist finding out. "What do you think?" I asked Tor.

120

"Personally, I would say we're better off understanding what kind of person he is. If Pax is right and we do need him, then we need to be aware what he's capable of. It'll cost us, but it's only a few hours."

"I agree. I hate the idea of taking a detour, but I need to know. Okay, let's get this done."

It took us over an hour to find Oliver's bunker. It was as Celeste had described it, the ground churned up, the doorway exposed and deformed, filled with rubble. Had it been a lucky hit? Or had the mech somehow known they were there? It seemed unlikely out here in the wilderness.

Tor took in the damage. "No way a mech did all of this. Some maybe, but not all. The door was already open. Celeste believed him because she wanted to."

"Do you think there are hundreds of these bunkers scattered throughout the province?" Hundreds of lives, human and cyborg alike, trapped, waiting, or dead beneath us as we walked over them.

Don't think about it.

Finding the bunker had been the easy part; the debris was going to take us hours to clear. My heart sank. "Tor, we can't. It's going to take us all day to move this." And we didn't have all day; only a few hours of weak light remained. "We're going to have to leave it. Why are you smiling?"

"Because," he said cheerfully, "it's my time to shine." He shucked off his pack and stripped down to his waist. "You may want to get out of the way." He winked.

"Did you just *wink* at me?" I asked as I stepped back. This was a side of him I hadn't seen yet.

He straightened his back, flexing his shoulders. I couldn't help but stare. It was obvious Tor had more strength than me. Sheer size aside, his cyberization had obviously been geared toward enhancing his already considerable physical strength. I'd experienced that firsthand. But I'd had no idea *how* strong he was.

He picked up the chunks of concrete and twisted metal like they were made of feathers, tossing them meters into the brush. His body...his skin was the golden olive of the South Sea pearls my mother had gotten as an anniversary gift from my father; not rare, but beautiful. He was like a sculpture come to life. Yes, he was corded with muscle, but it was more than that. He moved effortlessly, a seamless grace that belied his power.

The scars on his body were pale and smooth; like my own, they'd been mostly obliterated by the nanites, devoured and recycled into something useful. His past had been erased, a part of him I would never meet because it no longer existed. A fresh start was what we'd wanted, yet I couldn't help feeling like we'd lost something important.

I stood, absorbed in watching him, until it occurred to me to help. I chose a relatively smaller chunk and hoisted it as far as I could. It sailed through the trees, far beyond what I'd expected. Maybe I did have some super-strength after all. I lifted a heavier piece and flung it, marveling at the distance it covered before it slammed into a slender tree, causing it to shudder violently.

It was liberating. I'd been so ill for so long, I'd forgotten what it felt like to be normal, let alone healthy and fit. I'd been so overwhelmed from the time I'd woken up, I hadn't thought about it. I hadn't realized just how sick I'd actually been.

But look at me now.

I threw another large stone and screamed, just to hear the sound of my own voice. The noise startled Tor, causing him to fumble his chunk of rock, and I laughed.

"Enjoying yourself, are you?" He gave me a curious look.

I stretched my shoulders. "I'll explain to you later."

He removed the final stone blocking the entrance to the bunker, and a dark hole gaped before us. Once again, I doubted whether this was the right thing to do.

"Do you think I should try to see if anyone's down there? Like, with my mind? Just to be safe?"

Tor pushed on the warped doorframe, testing its strength. "Sure. It can't hurt."

I closed my eyes and searched for a thread, trying to let my instincts take over. *There.* I followed it and—

"But if we can create a brain and a body that mimic ours, what's left that makes us human? If the only thing that makes us human is our failings, what's the point of our existence?"

—*Della van Natta,* Artificial Life or Artificial Hope?

25
ROS

It was going to be today. I was ready. My heart knew it was the right choice.

I'd been a fool to think I could ever live without them. Even after everything they'd done to me, I couldn't do it. I couldn't stop loving them.

I couldn't live like this, underground, in a world with no sun and no hope. Simply waiting. For what? Mil and Lexa were talking in the hallway. They said they'd called the others home. I didn't know who these others were.

They said we were free now, able to live openly as we were. I didn't want that freedom. I wanted to be home, in my own bed, waking up to the odor of steaming dough and fresh chives. I wanted to argue with my mother about my unruly hair, hear her mourn the thickness of my waist.

I wanted my father to peer over his glasses and newspaper at me and ask me where I was going. I'd say the library, but we'd both know I was going to meet Julien. I wanted him to sigh and shake his head and wonder what would become of me.

Julien. I didn't love him then, but I did now. His crooked smile and bad-boy haircut. The way he knew I was too good for him.

Part of me wanted to leave here, to go and find them all. If anyone was strong enough to survive a war, it was my mother—purely out of spite, if nothing else. But I wasn't strong enough. I'd never been strong enough for anything. Not to be the woman my parents had wanted me to be, but not to be my own woman either. It was a simple truth: I wasn't able to survive.

A boy lived on the other side of my wall. Adrian. He was going to help me. We were going to help each other.

A soft tapping echoed on the wall next to my head. It was time.

"How would we choose who could become a cyborg? Surely you couldn't let just anyone do it. What if a psychopath wanted to become a cyborg? What then? You would practically be handing them the keys to the kingdom at that point. So, who's to say who could do it? Would the weak be given priority? The sick? Or would the choice go, as it so often does, to the highest bidder?"

—Derek Wills, Preserve Terra Society, 2039

26

AILITH

"Anything?" Tor's voice drew me back to the present, *our* present.

"I... No. I need to get back to her." I squeezed my eyes shut, as though that would make a difference. I wanted to push past the tightness in her throat, to stand in the empty place where her heart had been and anchor it there.

"Ailith!" Tor wrapped his fingers around my upper arms. "What's happening?"

"Something's wrong with her."

"With who? The woman in the bunker?"

"No. One of us. She's home. But she's... Oh, Tor. I've been in her before. She never wanted to become one of us. Her parents...and now she's—" My nails tore at the fabric of my coat.

"Ailith, stop." He crushed me to his chest, knocking the air out of me.

"Tor, her grief. I can't…we have to help her."

"Where is she?"

"She's home. We have to go home."

"Ailith, we don't know where 'home' is."

"She's one of us. I think she's going to do something. She—" I twisted in his arms, trying to break free. I may as well have tried to free myself from a stone.

"Ailith." His tone was conciliatory. "I know. I know you want to help her. But you can't be everywhere at once. And right now, you're here."

He was right, of course, but it wasn't what I wanted to hear.

"Look, we'll find her, I promise." His fingers were dry and dusty as they cupped my jaw, like my father's after a spring of planting potatoes. "Right now, we have to deal with what's in front of us. I'm not trying to be cruel, and I'm not going to pretend to understand how you, either of you, feel. But the only way to get to her is to keep moving forward. Yes?"

"Yes." I sounded petulant. But he was right. I searched for her thread again. It was dull, but it was still lit. For now. *Focus. He's right. We'll get there.*

He opened his arms tentatively, as though he were expecting me to run. "Are you good?"

I nodded. "Let's get this over with."

***

The air in the bunker was acrid and sour, and as cold as if we'd sunk into an icy lake. Tor tried the control panel set into the wall at the bottom of the stairs. To our surprise, the panel responded with a judder and whir, and a sickly yellow light filled the bunker. As soon as it had, I regretted it, regretted ever coming here.

Blood was everywhere, arcing in delicate sprays across the curved ceiling and walls. The room was different than it had been in my vision, the furniture overturned, shards of glass and colored enamel littering the floor. But I was sure.

"Tor, this is it. I've been here. In her."

I couldn't see her, even though the room was small. Not at first.

"Ailith, you'd better go outside," Tor said, his voice low.

"What? Why—" And there she was. In the corner of the room stood a standard service robot, a model so basic even the most cash-strapped households had one. They'd been built to avoid the uncanny valley altogether: their squat cylindrical shape was old-fashioned now, or rather, had been before the war.

Her head had been placed on top of the bot like a garish crown. She was perfectly preserved; not a hint of decomposition marked her skin. I remembered being inside her, her desperation at odds with the composed face before me. Black hair fell down the back of the robot. The onyx curls must have once been striking, but now they hung in lank, blood-soaked strands.

Tor swore under his breath in the language I'd found so comforting. I waited for my stomach to object, given how quickly it had surrendered before, but a faint grumble was all it mustered.

That's right, choose your battles.

We saw her body now, on its back in the bed, the lines visible through the thin linen. I didn't want to think about what else he may have done to her.

"Why does she look like that? Why hasn't she decomposed?" I whispered.

"It's pretty cold and dry down here. Is it definitely her? Is she familiar to you?" he asked.

"Yes. I remember her hair. Tor, he cut her head off."

"Well, he didn't lie about that part," he reminded me gently. "He did say he'd killed her. That she was infected with some kind of virus."

"Do you think that's true?"

"Do you?"

"She didn't feel infected. But there was something she had to do. I don't think it was a virus, though."

Tor was silent as he examined her remains. "No," he agreed. "I don't think so either. I would've found his story more believable if he hadn't placed her head there." He indicated the service bot. "Maybe she *was* up to something. But *that*, that's some kind of personal message. What the message is, probably only he knows for sure."

Is Tor speaking from personal experience? "What do we do?"

"Nothing. We don't have the tech to tell for sure whether or not she carried a virus. There's a small chance he's telling the truth."

"Tor? Do you think we—Could we resurrect her?" I remembered the man Oliver had brought back from the dead. Yes, he'd died afterward, but only because his body wasn't compatible with the nanites. Hers was.

Tor pressed his lips together. "No, I don't think we can. Not after this much time." He gave my shoulder a gentle squeeze.

"We should at least give her a funeral of some kind." I couldn't bear leaving her like that, her head standing sentry over her own corpse. Undignified and vulnerable.

"Well, we can't bury her. I could probably break through the permafrost, but I don't think these shovels will." He indicated the tools in the tiny storage cupboard.

"We'll burn her."

"Okay." He started toward her.

"No. No, Tor, let me. Please."

He hesitated as though he were about to protest, but he didn't. "If you're sure. I'll go and build a pyre. Ailith?" He turned back to me. "We can't stay to see her off. A fire might draw some unwanted attention."

I waited until Tor left the bunker before pulling the sheets off her body. The insides of her thighs seemed untouched. A small part of me was grateful. That he'd taken her life was bad enough, but at least he hadn't degraded her further.

Her body hadn't fared as well as her head. Her belly was soft and bloated. She'd clearly been a tall woman in life, but any curves she'd had were gone, soaked into the sheets with a sickly-sweet tang. Skin, flaking with dried blood, clung to her jutting hip bones, tiny splits opening over the sharpest peaks.

The water tank in the bunker was half full. I washed the evidence of violence from her body, although there was nothing I could do about the stump of her neck. An odd mark ringed her left thumb around the nail, as though the skin had been worn away.

I rubbed my thumbnail with my index finger, making quick circles.

I found a fresh sheet in the storage cupboard and laid it on the floor next to the bed. I lifted her body onto the sheet as gently as I could and crossed her arms over her stomach.

So far, so good. Now for her head.

I carefully washed her face then rinsed the blood from her hair and combed it out. She looked younger now, like a sleeping schoolgirl. I wished I could wake her up, ask for her version of events.

Does it even matter?

And then she opened her eyes.

No sense was left in me to scream. Only my fingers

130

moved, digging my nails into my palms.

It's not real. It's a fragment. A memory. It has to be.

Only, it wasn't. Her gaze crawled over me, searching for my face. When she found it, her mouth opened, and frozen, I waited for her to speak. Instead, she bit down, hard. Her jaws kept snapping, gnashing her teeth as though she would devour all the air in the room until only I was left and then she would consume me too.

As I stood, rooted to the spot, her teeth chipped and cracked, and her head teetered dangerously close to the edge of her pedestal. The idea of her head hitting the floor, the wet smack it would make, the grinding of her teeth against the concrete as she hunted me down finally woke me. I snatched a blood-streaked towel off the floor, ready to capture her when she toppled.

As suddenly as it had started, it stopped. Her eyes fell to half-mast, and her jaw slackened. I reached out to her in my mind, trying to find her thread. *There.* It disintegrated before I reached it, the fragments dissolving into nothingness. She was gone; this time, I was sure.

I wiped fragments of enamel off her lips then laid her head against the opening of her neck, draping her hair over the seam. I tried wrapping her the way I remembered the ancient mummies in museums, but since I hadn't had a lot of practice at this sort of thing, the result was clumsy.

Should I call Tor down for this part? He'd probably had experience wrapping bodies. *No. He might be insulted.*

I did the best I could, and finally, it was done.

***

"Are you going to tell me what happened down there?" Tor asked as we placed her body on the pyre and covered her with small sticks and handfuls of dried moss. I hadn't

131

said a word since we'd carried her body out of the bunker, but he'd seen the crescent-moon wounds on my palms.

"Nothing much. Just the usual visions." I forced a smile. *I just can't. I'd like to stave off losing my mind for as long as possible, thank you very much.*

"Should we say something?"

I couldn't think of anything to say that didn't sound trite. "I wish we'd known you in life." It was true, at least, even if it wasn't altruistic. If we'd met her when she was alive, we would've been able to tell if Oliver had told us the truth, and we would've had a better idea of what kind of man he was: savior or monster.

We held hands as she burned, the smoke twisting up through the bones of the forest. I tried again to reach out to Pax. His thread felt patchy; he must've been sleeping. Considering what they were going through, it was best to let him. It wasn't like I had good news to give them anyway.

"Ailith? We have to go." Tor had stayed longer than he'd wanted, for me.

He was right; we couldn't stay here.

As we left the clearing, the presence again made itself felt, the one that had been following us.

Him.

Whoever was following us was a person. He may have been hidden, but I *felt* him, far back in the woods, watching.

"I will stand guard."

The voice sounded in my head; the elusive thread flared. *"Who are you?"*

Nothing. The thread withdrew.

"Thank you," I whispered, hoping the smoke carried my message to him.

We'd walked for barely twenty minutes when two of my threads began to flicker.

132

"The creation of cyborgs is, without a doubt, one of the vilest actions of the 21st century. The purpose of creating artilects is to birth a perfect being, uncontaminated by human frailties and failings. To dilute that perfection by polluting it with the very characteristics we're trying to raise the human race above is an insult to the very nature of our intelligence and goals for humanity."

—Ethan Strong, Novus Corporation, 2039

27

ADRIAN

The android's voice echoed in my head. Over and over, she spoke to me.

"You are very handsome."

The nanites were inside me, breaking me open, climbing inside and devouring me. I was becoming like her, one cell at a time.

It wasn't supposed to happen this way. They'd told me I would still be human. They'd lied. I wasn't human. I never would be. No one would ever be human again. How could they?

A strength was growing inside me; I was afraid of it. What good came of having this much strength if I had no free will? They were talking in the hallway about how they'd activated the signal to call the others 'home.' If they could do that, make us come when they called, what else could they do? Or have us do?

I couldn't become like her. Vulnerable, programmed to obey someone else's wishes.

The blankness of her eyes as I pushed myself into her, her moans perfectly timed to my thrusts.

Connections had formed in my mind, like a giant spider web around my brain. Connections that shouldn't have existed. They were right to start a war over us.

Ros, the girl in the room next door to mine, was crying. Our beds must've been pushed together, only the thin wall separating us. I'd seen her when she'd first arrived: her hair dark and silky, her almond-shaped eyes red-rimmed, her body doubled over as though she were in pain. She'd barely stopped crying since we'd woken up.

Three days ago, I'd told her my plan. I needed to share it with someone. She wouldn't betray me. In fact, she was going to come with me. I was glad; I didn't want to go alone. But I needed to go now, while I could. They were giving us our space, letting us 'adjust.' They were also distracted, waiting for the others to return. I hoped the others wouldn't come here, that they would die on the way. I wouldn't wish this life on anyone.

I'd been practicing in the privacy of my room, and I'd come to a conclusion: killing a cyborg was difficult. We couldn't be poisoned or drowned, and it would take us a long time to starve to death. Too long. We regenerated from most wounds; the nanites rebuilt us. Our bionic components made it difficult to break our bones, even our necks. I'd tried.

Our deaths had to be swift, and they had to be catastrophic.

We'd found kerosene in the storage room, along with years of stockpiled supplies. Had they known what was going to happen? The war and the aftermath?

We told Mil and Lexa we were going for a walk. They seemed relieved; they believed we were finally coming to terms with our new life. I hated myself for betraying their trust, but they'd done this to us. They'd been part of everything since the beginning.

I expected the sun would come out for us, to define our final moments in brilliance. It didn't. The world stayed cold and uncaring, too wrapped up in its own death.

The kerosene burned our skin and made our eyes water. Her

hands were so delicate, her nail beds ragged from her tiny teeth. The soaked fabric of my trousers clung to me in cold creases, chilling me as we knelt.

Would it hurt? Would the nanites run from us, bursting through our cells like animals fleeing a forest fire?

It did hurt. At first. Then it hurt so badly it became nothing. Our hands were permanently entwined; I couldn't let go of her even if I'd wanted to. A gasp pulsed through my brain, as though someone was trying to breathe for me. It was too late.

We were finally free.

"It's naïve to think for one minute that publicly banning the creation of artilects will stop their creation, especially in this climate of global competition. The benefits of artilect creation to the economy, to political prestige, to sheer scientific curiosity will ensure that the push for their creation will continue. The only effect the ban will have will be to remove the transparency of the process and push the movement underground, where it cannot be regulated and will be controlled by finances and competition, rather than ethics."

—Della van Natta, *Artificial Life or Artificial Hope?*

28
AILITH

The two threads went dark.

I couldn't stop them. I tried to force my way in, to move their hands, to make them throw the canister, to force their lungs to blow out the flames. I failed.

I want to follow them.

I could no longer live here, in this life. I was a shadow, lost in the ether. Done.

His hands were on me, a tether. It wouldn't be enough. *He* wouldn't be enough.

In the darkness, a new thread. A lifeline.

"...the most difficult aspect for the sentience of our artilect blueprint has been emotion. Not the expression of it, but the feel of it for the artilect. It's the one area of the human brain we've had difficulty replicating. We can program responses to a million possible variables, sure, but our goal is to have artilects truly feel it. Currently, we use images specifically provocative to the human brain to induce an automatic response, in hopes that the machine will be able to eventually translate these into something meaningful for itself..."

—Robin Leung, CEO of Novus Corporation, 2039

29
FANE

I must've been dreaming, if I could dream. She ran across an endless field, the sky open and clear. She was only a child, clutching the end of my leash in her tiny fist as her slight body cut through the long grass like an arrow. I was trapped in a metal cage, my arms and legs trailing uselessly as she pulled me along. She'd tied ribbons to me to make me less frightening, but I was the frightened one. And yet, I would've followed her anywhere.

We raced toward the tree, always our destination. It took us a long time—when we reached it, she was a woman grown. He was waiting by the tree for her, as always. My body became tangled in the branches; I couldn't set myself free. She would come for me. She always did. I wanted to warn her about the bark—her skin was fragile and easily damaged—but I was too late, and her skin peeled away. She ignored the blood and reached for me, her fingers trembling.

She wasn't gentle. When she caught hold of me at last, she squeezed, too hard. I cried out, but my voice was gone. All that came was a gust of wind, blowing gently through her hair. We climbed back down and, as always, he was gone. Where did he go? Why didn't he wait longer for us? She lay on the ground, her face pressed into the dirt. I was forgotten, propped up against the base of the tree. The infinite field became my only horizon as I waited for her to return. As always.

"I know many of you believe that by enhancing humans with robotic and artilectual components, we feel we are creating gods. Let me assure you, this is false. The purpose, the sole purpose, of creating true cyborgs is to follow the natural and logical progression of the human race. Both the Terrans and the Cosmists must be satisfied; the Terrans because our humanity will not be replaced, and the Cosmists because we are conveying the human race far beyond its expected potential."

—*Lexa Gillet, Pantheon Modern Cyborg Symposium, 2040*

30
AILITH

I vomited. My stomach had always been a coward. "They're gone. I couldn't stop them. They're just…gone."

"Ailith, who's gone? I don't—"

"The others. Like us. The ones who are home. They burned themselves alive." My voice sounded muffled in my ears, as though I was far underground. "Tor, we need to go home."

"If people are killing themselves there, perhaps we shouldn't be trying to find it." His mouth was a thin line. I was proving his suspicions right.

"No. You don't understand." I gave up. I couldn't explain it to him. Not in a way he'd comprehend. Not yet.

"Ailith, look, I'm not saying we won't go to this home. I'm saying we need to be careful. One thing at a time. Agreed?"

"Agreed."

We'd gone only a few miles before I tired. My stamina wasn't as augmented as Tor's to begin with, and everything that had happened in the last twenty-four hours pulled like a weight on my chest. But we couldn't stop; we shouldn't even slow down. We needed to travel as far as possible before it got even darker. Tor noticed me lagging behind and waited for me to catch up.

"Are you okay?"

"I—" The bunker. The visions. *He was so excited about becoming a cyborg and so disgusted by what he'd become. She just wanted her parents to love her.* Their loss was as deep as if I'd known them, not just been a passenger for brief moments of their lives.

Tor fumbled in his pack for the map, pretending he didn't see the tears threatening behind my eyes. As he studied it, a slow smile spread across his face.

"How do you feel about a quick detour? A *quick* one. We need to rest, Ailith, or we won't be any use to them by the time we get there," he insisted as I opened my mouth to protest.

I shut it. I was too tired to argue.

Half an hour later, as the sky deepened from dark gray to black, Tor motioned for me to stand still while he disappeared down into the gloom. The air here was oddly humid; a fine mist wreathed the trees. Below, the orange glow of a fire flared into life. Tor returned a few minutes later.

"Close your eyes." He was obviously pleased with himself, a shy smile curving his mouth. We descended through the fog, the damp air thick and harder to breathe. It was also warm. I took a deeper breath and tasted minerals, and something else I couldn't identify.

"Stand here," he instructed me.

140

"What is this?" I couldn't help smiling. It must be a good thing, and I needed a good thing right now.

"Open your eyes." He gestured grandly. "Your bath, madam."

It was a hot spring, a small pool of water heated naturally by the ground. I'd visited places like this on holiday when I was a child, staying up hours past bedtime to float on my back and count the stars. Those pools had been huge and commercial, entire towns built around them. Here there was nothing but rocks and steep cliff faces.

I knew Tor was trying to make me feel better, but it was bittersweet. The last time I'd been to a hot spring, my entire family had still been alive.

I dropped my pack. "I can't believe no one's holed up here. It seems pretty ideal, especially in this weather."

"I was wondering that myself. Maybe someone did. But, there's definitely no one here now. Or recently, for that matter."

"It seems too good to be true," I said warily.

Tor laughed. "Enjoy yourself for a few minutes. You can worry again in an hour."

No arguments here. I stripped off my clothes as quickly as I could, my skin prickling with the cold.

I slid into the water up to my neck, and a sudden, painful tingle gripped my entire body, squeezing my ribs and blocking my throat. Tor grabbed at his chest, the muscles in his neck taut with strain.

"Tor?"

As quickly as it had come, the sensation disappeared, leaving nothing but a gentle warmth in its wake.

"Probably just the heat of the water after so long in the cold air," I said.

"Yeah. It caught me off guard." He examined the

141

surface of the water, as though he wasn't convinced.

This pool wasn't quite as warm as I'd remembered, but it was warm enough to make my toes ache as they thawed. Sweat and grime dissolved from my skin as I floated; the tension in my muscles did not.

Tor was right. I needed to enjoy myself, to have some kind of release. More than a hot bath offered. I'd seen the way he stared at me when I stepped into the water. He may have only gotten a peek, but he'd liked what he saw. Maybe it was a mistake, but right now, I needed something. *Him.* Besides, we might be dead tomorrow. Or the next day. Hell, no day in the foreseeable future looked good for us.

I would have to make the first move—I knew Tor well enough now to realize that—but he wanted me. He looked at me too long, held his breath when I brushed against him. Said my name whenever he could and built our shelters way too small.

I'm on to you.

Tor had lowered himself onto one of the seats hewn into the rock around the pool. His head leaned back against the cold stone; his eyes were closed.

Deep breath.

I straddled him, my hands on either side of his head. He arched in surprise beneath me as I kissed his exposed throat, but didn't protest.

"Ailith—"

I covered his lips with mine. He became hard beneath me, and I moaned against his mouth, urging him on, crushing the droplets of steam beading on his skin with my fingertips. He explored my body, slowly, against the resistance of the water.

When his fingers finally found their way inside me, I was ready.

"Tor." My voice was a low feral sound I'd never heard

before.

He wrapped his hands around my waist and lifted me until my feet found purchase against the stone shelf. He spread me with his fingers and devoured me, licking and sucking until the rising flood inside me overflowed and I came. As I cried out, he drove his tongue deep inside me, coaxing me to another climax. I ground against his mouth, my hands buried in his hair.

He raised himself out of the water to the worn stones at its edge, and in one swift motion lifted me onto his lap. I wrapped my legs around his waist, sliding onto him and taking him inside me all at once. His body held more heat for me than the water, and I was warm for the first time since I'd woken up.

A low groan rumbled from deep inside his throat as I rode him, his hands clutching at my hips, rocking himself deeper inside me. His fingers knotted in my hair, and he pressed our foreheads together as he came.

To: [————————--]
From: [————————--]

July 30, 2040

I can confirm that Pantheon Modern Corporation Cyborg Program Omega-117 has been a success. Confirmation of survival absolute. Recommend instigation of protocol Theta-626, effective immediately.

31

FANE

Ji burst through the door, breathless, his face flushed. My anticipation was white sheets of paper, a blank screen. Hope, tiny green leaves pushing through the black soil to welcome the sun.

"They've done it." *He gulped in air, shaking his head as his mother rose from her seat, her eyes flashing.*

"They've done what, exactly?" *she asked, although she knew the answer as well as the rest of us.*

"Cyborgs. The true ones. And some of them survived."

We'd known this day was coming, yet all but myself were shocked. I was pleased, a bird soaring over a lake in the blazing sun, the iridescent scales on a fish as it twisted in the air to catch a fly. The color yellow. This was the beginning I'd been waiting for.

Some of them were revolted. Like most Cosmists, they saw these cyborgs as an abomination, the corruption of a pure concept. Diluted gods. They'd tried everything in their power to prevent them from being created. Terrible things. And still they'd failed.

144

Ethan spat on the floor. "What a fucking waste. All that time, money, effort. For fuck's sake." Stella put her hand on his arm, but he brushed her off. "Do you have any idea how much this will set us back? Wasted resources aside? We could be dead in the water."

Dead in the water. Floating on their backs, gray and bloated, their eyes eaten away.

"Maybe it won't. Maybe it'll be a good thing for us," Stella said.

"Really, Stella? Really? What in fuck makes you think this could ever be a good thing?"

Stella usually remained silent when Ethan shouted at her. She glanced at me, and I smiled, hoping it would give her courage. It did.

"Why do you assume they'll be against us? Maybe they'll stand with us. They'll act as a bridge, making it easier for us to do what we're doing. And if everything does go to shit, think what effective soldiers they'd make. All that power, which we could control."

"Yes, all that power used against us. Why would you believe they'll choose a side? They'll be their own side, using their power against us to preserve themselves. They will destroy us. Cyborgs don't want us to create artilects any more than the Terrans do; it would knock them lower on the food chain. And as for cyborgs being effective soldiers? Seriously? Soldiers with the power of artilects but with the ability to make their own choices? You want efficient killers? Then we keep trying to build artilects. Fuck!"

A long pause followed his declaration. Everyone was staring at me.

"What do you think?" Stella asked.

"I think it's wonderful," I replied honestly. "I can't wait to meet them."

I didn't feel the same way most of them did about artilects. While I shared their desire to create life, I didn't believe that artilects were akin to gods. Nor were their creators. But to Ethan, and many of the others, that was their gospel, their religion. Creating a fully sentient artilect was their opus, their way of ensuring their immortality not only on this earth, but across the galaxy.

145

And like others before them, they would crush those who stood in their way.

I didn't agree with him, but I understood his bitterness at being so close to everything he'd ever wanted.

Bitterness. Marigold petals. A heaviness at the back of my throat.

"Meet them? Christ." Ethan covered his face with his hands. "We're not going to meet them. We're going to find a way to destroy them. We can't let them live."

"Why not?"

"Why? Haven't you been listening? They threaten everything we've been working toward. It took us ten years longer than it should have to get where we are. Not only did they suck up valuable resources, but they've also freaked everybody the fuck out. It wasn't so bad, an artificial leg here, a plastic heart there, but that's not what these cyborgs are. They look human, but every cell, every goddamn cell in their body's been cyberized. Do you know what that makes them?"

I did. I knew very well.

"Don't speak to Fane like that!" Lien approached Ethan, her eyes blazing.

"Lien, he needs to understand. They threaten us by their very existence. And aside from that, they're disgusting."

Disgusting. Maggots crawling over the body of a dead kitten. A finger breaking through the skin of an overripe fruit.

"I do understand. The cyborgs will survive."

"Not if we have anything to do with it, they won't. In fact, it's time we started on Plan B." With a last shake of his head, Ethan turned on his heel and left the room.

The others filed after him.

Only Lien remained. She put her hand on my arm. "Ignore him. He's angry because he wanted more for us."

I didn't think it was that simple; there was more to it than that. Something more dangerous. A very great height, a dark alley. A broken heart.

Plan B was a secret. They kept things from me; they didn't trust

146

me. But whatever Plan B was, it wouldn't be good. Someone would die. Someone always died.

Lien appraised my face in a way I didn't like. Hands fisting in my hair. Something crawling over my skin. Arms trying to cover my shame. They'd been getting longer, these looks. Most of them looked at me like that.

Her fingers were papery, dry. They made me want to peel off my own skin, to become someone else.

I shrank away from her without meaning to, and I was sorry as soon as I did. They needed to be on my side right now. Especially her.

Her eyes narrowed, but she let it pass. She believed I was disturbed by what Ethan had said. She was right. She gave me a last long stare then left the room.

I traced the shape of tiny leaves on my palm. Maybe these new cyborgs would help me, or maybe they would be afraid of me, of what I represented to them. I hoped not. I wanted them to like me.

Something was coming, teasing me from somewhere inside my own brain. It was like wind rushing around me. A vast, emerald sea.

"In the same week as global legislation banned the creation of artilects, just weeks before Novus Corporation was scheduled to create the first true artilect, millions of machines around the world have been malfunctioning. Is it a passive-aggressive sulk triggered by their creators, a silent protest of the ban? Or is it, as some conspiracy theorists have suggested, something more sinister?"

—Shirley Novak, CNN Tech Watch, 2040

32

AILITH

I woke up as the sky lightened into rose-quartz gray. Wisps of images still clung to me.

White paper. Marigold petals. The endless green field.

I'd been asleep for only a few hours, Tor less than that. He'd watched me for a while after he'd thought I'd gone to sleep.

But, between the tiny amount of sleep I'd managed and the physical release of sex in general, and with Tor in particular, I was revitalized. He still slept, more deeply than I'd ever seen him.

"Pax? Can you hear me?"

"Ailith? Are you here?"

"No, but we're close. But we couldn't convince Oliver to come with us, Pax."

"He has to be here."

"I know, but—"

The reason this hot spring had been abandoned was clear at last.

What I'd believed to be rocks were, in fact, corpses.

Many of them, human and animal, radiating out from around the pool.

I bit the back of my hand so I wouldn't scream.

"Ailith? Ailith! Ai—"

"Tor!" I gave his shoulder a violent shake. In seconds, he was awake and on his feet, the hunter in him ready to fight.

"Ailith? Are you okay?"

Wordlessly, I pointed at the spread of bodies.

Tor inhaled sharply, his eyes wide. He walked over to the carcass closest to him, a tiny caribou calf, and knelt beside it. As he ran his hands over its body, the pressure of his fingers shifted the frail bones beneath its molting pelt. Finding nothing, he peered into its eyes and mouth.

"What the hell happened?" I asked, my voice wavering.

Tor's voice was steady. "The water. Remember the sensation when we first got in? *That's* why no one lives here. The water must be poisoned with something you wouldn't even have to drink. I should've known. It's an old trick."

"How can you be so calm?" I hated the sharp edge of hysteria in my voice. "We could've died!"

Tor shook his head. "I don't think we were ever in any real danger. And I'm not calm." It was true; his hands were trembling. "Are you okay?" he asked.

"Well, I'm better off than them." An insane urge to giggle bubbled up inside me "I can't imagine rabbits drinking from hot springs."

"Hares. And I don't think they did." Tor scraped up some of the dirt around the pool and rubbed it between his fingers. "I think the ground's been poisoned. The hares

149

and caribou ate whatever plants they found, and everything else ate them."

"What about those people?" I asked, pointing at the huddle of human corpses. Without the interference of insects, their skin had desiccated into thick leather kept supple by the steam. It clung to their bones and bared their teeth to the cold air. Their eyes stared blankly at the sky, the whites black and shriveled.

"Most likely they were poisoned by the water. Probably couldn't believe their luck when they found this place."

"Why would someone do this?"

He rubbed the markings on his forehead. "It was a war, Ailith. Believe me, this isn't the worst thing I've seen."

I believed him. "We need to bury them somehow. We should—"

"Ailith? Are you there? Are you all right?"

Pax.

"Yes, we're fine. We just… It's a long story. Listen, we're coming. Soon."

"He must come with you."

"Tor? Of course."

"No. The other. He must come with you."

"Oliver? Pax, he refused. He's not coming."

"He has to. If he doesn't, we won't succeed. Everything will fail."

"What do you mean? Pax, he's not going to—"

"He must." Pax sounded frantic now, his fear physically palpable in my mind. Images flashed through it. Myself, Tor, people I didn't recognize. Screaming, the wet sounds of people dying, and the taste of metal in the fine red mist that hung over all of us. Then, nothing. Only the world remained, silent and still.

"Pax, what is this? What am I seeing?"

"The future."

"Will Oliver prevent this from happening, Pax? Is that it?"

"He must come." And then he was gone.

"Tor, we *need* Oliver. Pax showed me the future. If Oliver doesn't come, everyone will die." I rested my face in my hands. Tor's warmth inside me was a distant memory now.

Tor chewed at his lower lip. "So, if we don't arrive with Oliver, there's going to be a bloodbath?"

"That's what it looked like. Tor…all those people, dead."

"How does Pax know all this?"

"You're probably tired of hearing this, but I don't know. It *felt* true. Maybe that's his thing—seeing the future."

He dragged his hand down his face. "Right. Why not? Well, I guess we've got no choice then. It looks like we're going back to the Saints of Loving Grace."

"But how are we going to convince Oliver to come with us? Are we going to call his bluff?"

"No," said Tor, "we're going to join the game."

We laid the bodies together, side-by-side, and covered them with shale and rocks in a kind of makeshift cairn. It wasn't ideal, but it was the best we could do. I wanted to promise that we would come back and give them the burial they deserved, but it would've been a lie.

We turned back the way we'd come. Without any detours, the trip back to the village would be fast. Pax's voice had had a different quality this time, a lucidity that only comes with pain. I recognized it from my own voice, before my transformation.

As we marched, we tried to formulate a plan. With any luck, Tor's strategy of gaming Oliver would work.

"We have to make it clear to him that no one is to be killed. That we only want to get Pax and Cindra out. Ideally, no one will get as much as a splinter. We need to avoid that

151

future at all costs."

"I agree it's ideal, Ailith, but it's not realistic. What if they fight back? Do you think they're going to allow us to saunter in and take them with us? They'll probably want to capture us as well. What do we do then? Surrender?"

"No, of course not. But when they see there are more of us... Or maybe we should sneak in and steal them back?"

"That would be a good idea if we knew anything about the camp. But we don't. Haven't they been kept in some kind of building the whole time? That's what I would've done, if I were holding them captive. Kept them inside so they had no idea where they were. After a while, even if they did manage to escape, they would be too confused to go far." From the authority in his voice, it was clear he spoke from experience.

"Okay, so we may have to confront them. But nobody needs to get hurt."

"Ailith, they kidnapped Pax and Cindra. They're holding them against their will. They're *torturing* them. Convincing them to let two cyborgs just walk out might be difficult. But I happen to agree with you."

"You do?" I didn't mean to sound surprised, but I was. "I just thought—"

"What? Once a killer, always a killer?"

Well, yes.

He must've seen the answer in my face because he stopped walking. Gripping me gently by the chin, he gazed into my eyes. "Ailith, the whole reason I became what we are was so I could stop killing. When I became a cyborg, I vowed I would never take a human life ever again, even in self-defense. Of course, that was before I found myself in this wasteland, but it still stands. I will never go back to that life. If I did, I would lose what little soul I have left."

I smiled at him and gave him a quick kiss on the chin. "Could we trade something for them? Like medicine? Or food?"

"I don't think we have enough of either to tempt them. Especially not if they think our nanites are going to cure them. We'll have to see what happens when we get there. We'll scope the place out, see if we can't snatch them if they bring them above ground. Or, one of us can distract them, while the other two spirit them away. Oliver's a fast talker—it may just work. And if all else fails, we'll use some good old-fashioned intimidation." His optimism was catching.

And not like him at all. I almost expected him to start whistling.

"Are you okay?" I asked him.

"Yes. Why? What do you mean?"

"You're so...cheerful."

"Why wouldn't I be? It seems that nearly everyone on the planet—well, everyone in our part of it, anyway—is dead. There's no sun, no food, we have to walk everywhere, and we're about to beg a madman to help us break two unknown cyborgs out of a Terran stronghold. And—" He held up a hand as I rolled my eyes. "I have you. What more could I want?"

*"God created Man
Man destroyed God
Man created God
God destroyed Man"*

—*Terran protest chant, 2040*

33
CALLUM

My heart beat so hard my throat ached.

Keep still. Just keep your head down.

I was in the library, as far back into its depths as I could go. I'd gotten here a half hour ago to connect to one of the ports. I didn't know my way around it very well. I'd only come in because I was looking for some information the university deemed too sensitive to put on the internet.

The music blaring through my headphones was so loud I almost hadn't heard the explosions. They were just muffled booms, and I hadn't thought much of it until I'd glanced up and everyone had disappeared, including the librarian. I'd turned down the volume just as another one rippled through the silent room. Faint screams followed.

Terran extremists. It had to be. The ones who'd been protesting outside the university the last few weeks, railing against the developments the Advanced Artificial Intelligence Studies course was making. My course.

Another explosion had sounded, this one closer. I'd quickly

154

packed up my bag and backed away toward the recesses of the paper archives, keeping my eyes on the door. I could hear footsteps in the hallway, running. Then another explosion, and they were silent.

No way. I'd come so far, had just gotten what I'd wanted for so long, and now I was going to die.

Yesterday, I couldn't believe where my life was going. Even though my hand had been trembling, I'd still made out the tiny CONGRATULATIONS at the top of the page, accepting me into the program at Pantheon Modern.

It had been my lucky year, although if I were honest with myself, it wasn't merely luck. I'd worked hard to get where I was. But still, I'd never imagined I'd get accepted to both the cyborg program and the advanced AI course at the university.

I'd been at the university for only six months, but the choice had been a no-brainer. No way would I have turned the Pantheon Modern program down. Why study artificial intelligence when you could practically become one yourself? University had been a fallback for me. The only real question had been whether to tell my parents now or wait until after I'd been through the process and then surprise them.

Not that it had mattered, either way. Their reaction was predictable. My mom would hug me and say, "That's wonderful!" My father would clap me on the back. Two minutes later, they'd be buried back in their work, anything I'd said a distant memory. It wasn't that they didn't care; they were just very busy. Like me, they studied artificial intelligence. It didn't leave room for much else.

I'd even been raised by a robot nanny, one of the first of her kind. She'd done everything my parents would've done: read to me, played with me, tucked me in at night. When her body had failed about three years ago, I'd had her made portable. Right now, she resided in my laptop.

I patted it through my bag. "Don't worry, Umbra, we'll be okay."

I'd been so excited. She was the first one I'd told. "What do you think, Umbra? Can you believe it?"

"You've worked very hard. You deserve it, and I'm proud of you,"

155

she'd said, her voice smooth and almost human, thanks to the reprogramming I'd done on her last year. Before that, she'd spoken haltingly, her cadence stilted and formal.

"I guess I'd better start on my withdrawal letter, eh?"

"Perhaps you should consider staying at the university."

"What? What do you mean? You know how badly I've wanted this."

"Perhaps it would be safer if you stayed at the university."

"Safer? Safer for who?" At first, the activists had been content to chant mantras and wave placards, but a week ago, things had turned ugly. Labs had been broken into and equipment destroyed; some of my classmates had been assaulted.

And now, it seemed, they'd taken their protest to the next level. Had people been killed? If so, how many? I had no idea where they were; it was best to stay put and wait it out. Better to remain here where I would know if anyone came in than run into them in the hallway.

I wished I'd already become a cyborg. Then I could find whoever was doing this and face them head-on, maybe save someone. But I wasn't a cyborg, not yet.

"The procedure for becoming a cyborg is risky," Umbra had said.

"Yeah, but it couldn't be a huge risk, otherwise they wouldn't be doing it at all, right?"

I'd been sworn to secrecy on the exact nature of the process, but of course, I'd told Umbra. It was so exciting, a completely new generation of cyborg, more advanced than anything we were thinking about at the university.

Besides, I was willing to take any risk if it meant becoming a cyborg. The fact that it would be totally awesome aside, I truly believed it would help with situations like the protestors. Once they saw how seamlessly biology and technology integrated, how it would only enhance what they already were, they couldn't possibly be against it.

Umbra and I had talked about the Terrans at length for months.

"Whether they like it or not, Umbra, this is just the way the world

156

is heading. *Artificial intelligence, sentient artificial intelligence, is going to happen, and sooner than they think. They're only fighting the inevitable."*

"*They believe artilects will make humans obsolete, maybe even threaten your extinction,*" Umbra had replied.

"*Well, thanks to popular media, people assume artilects will be evil and enslave the human race.*"

"*Callum, they think the same about cyborgs,*" she'd reminded me.

It was true. Not the ones with biomechatronics, but the ones who had enhancements they didn't need. The Terrans interpreted it as though cyborgs were arming themselves over regular humans. They worried the cyborgs and artilects would team up and destroy them.

"*They say cyberization will make us no longer human. They would shit a brick if they knew what Pantheon Modern was up to. So would the Cosmists,*" I'd said.

When I became a cyborg, I'd show them how non-threatening it was. And how wonderful. There were so many amazing things about it that they didn't seem to see. Integrating ourselves with machines would preserve our humanity, not threaten it. We would live longer, be able to do more, go further. In fact, the way things were going in the world, it might be the only way for humanity to survive.

More footsteps sounded in the hallway, heavy, booted feet pounding in unison as they ran. Far down the hallway there was a roar, the crack of gunfire, a scream. Then nothing. I started toward the front door.

"*Area clear. Target down,*" a voice said on the other side.

A transcom crackled into life. "*Copy that. Move out.*"

I released the breath I'd been holding. I was safe. I could still become a cyborg, and then they'd see. Everyone, Terrans and Cosmists alike. It wouldn't be long now until they understood how important this time in history was for us all.

"I don't know what the big deal is, Ed. I'd personally love an artilect husband. Works all day, never complains, has lots of stamina where it counts, if you get what I mean. Maybe that's the problem, Ed. Maybe it's just men worrying that they're going to be replaced by a superior model."

—Shirley Novak, CNN Tech Watch, 2039

34
AILITH

We crested the hill beside the Saints of Loving Grace early the next morning. The loudspeaker calling the parishioners to service cleared the latest thread from my mind. The boy in the university library, Callum, was a new one. Where was he now? He must've become a cyborg and still be alive if I could inhabit him.

"Nice timing," Tor remarked.

It was. For Tor's plan to work, we needed as many of them present as possible. "Are you ready?"

"Showtime."

Oliver's face was like thunder as we burst through the door at the back of the hall, interrupting whatever exalted ramblings he'd planned for that day. Every other head in the room turned toward us, their eyes wide with shock.

Celeste, in her usual post as close to Oliver as she could manage, was the first to react. "Ailith!" she called, genuine joy on her face.

Oliver rushed down the center aisle toward us, his hand

knotted into fists. "What are you doing here?" His façade slipped, and his voice dripped with venom. "I told you never to come back."

"Go," Tor told me.

I hurried back the way Oliver had come, toward the pulpit at the head of the room. Oliver grabbed at my arm as I passed, but Tor stepped casually between us, sweeping him up in the bear hug of old friends. As strong as Oliver may have been, he was no match for Tor, and there was nothing he could do short of assaulting another god in front of their worshippers.

Once I reached the pulpit, I raised my hands to silence the buzzing crowd. I tried to appear as beatific and ethereal as possible, my face calm and serene. "Members of the Saints of Loving Grace, you have always been unwavering in your belief in us. Your piety has made our very existence possible, for without you, we would have no reason to exist. I—"

Tor widened his eyes and inclined his head, indicating that I'd better hurry the hell up.

"I am sorry, then, to pass along some troubling news. You have already met three of us, survivors of the apocalypse that you, in your wisdom, predicted was coming. There are, in fact, two more of us." There was an initial gasp of delight amongst the crowd then a muttering as it dawned on them that I wasn't announcing good news.

"It seems they have been taken captive by a group of Terrans, whom you know do not feel the way you do about us. We wish to ask for your assistance in freeing them. We have no desire to bring violence upon them, no matter what they have done. We are hoping that by the sheer force of our numbers and power of our faith, they will see sense and release them. Will you help us?"

Silence weighed heavily on the room before it erupted

159

into chaos. Everyone spoke at once, their voices rising in a furious crescendo over our heads. Tor finally stepped out of Oliver's way, and he sprinted to the pulpit.

Is he going to hit me?

He didn't. Instead, he raised his hands and addressed the crowd, entreating them to be quiet. As the roar died to a scattering of whispers, he spoke. "Please, I know what you have heard is disturbing." He shot me a glare that promised a world of pain. "But this is a matter between us artlects. We do not need you to get involved."

"But Ailith said—"

I was surprised to see Celeste standing before the crowd, her voice steady and strong as she faced Oliver.

"I heard what Ailith said. But there is no way we can retrieve the other…artlects without risking *your* lives. And I am not willing to do that. You have seen what these Terrans are capable of. Look at what they did to the world. You might all die." He slashed his hand through the air.

"No." I stepped in front of Oliver. "I believe we can save them without any violence on either side. That the mere sight of you and your faith will be enough to sway them. I understand your Divine is trying to protect you. He *is* noble like that."

Another death stare.

"Don't make me call your bluff," I whispered, so low only he heard me.

Something in his face changed then, and we'd won.

All eyes turned reflexively toward Oliver, awaiting his decision.

"You'll regret this," he whispered back then stepped forward to the edge of the dais. "We will go and help the other artlects. I shall meet now with Ailith and Tor and decide on a plan of action. You are all dismissed for now. I will call for you to gather when we have decided."

I walked among the crowd as they hurried out of the hall, eager to obey Oliver's wishes. Many of them chattered excitedly to each other, and I regretted deceiving them. But no harm would come to them, and we needed them. I just hoped this gamble would pay off. A small hand slid into mine, and I turned to see Celeste, her face pink with elation.

"Oh, Ailith, isn't it exciting! We're actually going to be part of something. No longer standing by as the world changes around us. We're finally seizing our destiny and *taking action*."

"Surely you won't be going?" I asked, surprised. In our plan, only the men and women, *adult* men and women, would be participating.

She faltered. "What? But why? I have as much faith as anyone."

"Oh, Celeste, I know." I touched her arm. "But you're so young and—"

"I survived as well as everyone else, didn't I?" Her face flushed a deep scarlet.

"Of course you have. It's only… I'm trying to protect you."

Her face softened a bit. "But *we* should be protecting *you*. It's our fate."

Fucking Oliver. I hoped the faith these people had in him was justified. Not that I was any better.

When everyone had left the hall, Oliver took us to his living quarters. Each of the men in the village had their own residence, while the woman lived together in the large house in the center. His home was more modest than I'd expected, but perhaps that was part of his disguise.

Was he living up to their expectations of what an artilect god was? Or had they adjusted their beliefs accordingly? If his house was anything to go by, the Saints were unsure of

161

Oliver's level of sentience. His house had been decorated sufficiently to reflect someone with likes and dislikes, but with enough austerity to suit a tenant who had little emotional attachment to such things.

The door crashed shut behind us.

"What the fuck do you think you're doing? I told you not to come back. I told you what would happen if you did."

"I don't believe you. I don't think you would ever hurt these people. After all, who would stroke your ego if you killed them all?"

"But why did you come back? I understood we'd reached an agreement..."

"Pax, one of the cyborgs we need to rescue, insists that we need you to be successful." Maybe I could appeal to his ego.

"Bullshit. It's a fucking trap. Doesn't the whole thing seem a bit shady to you? Surely you see it?" he addressed Tor.

Tor glanced from me to him, his eyes wary. "Yes, it does. But," he continued as I started to protest, "we do have reason to believe it's not."

"How do you even know you're talking to another cyborg? Maybe you're talking to yourself." He sneered at me.

"Look, this is happening. Unless you want your followers to see how full of it you are. Do you think they'll continue to follow a god who stood by as others were tortured and killed? Not to mention, if Pax and Cindra are fallible, it means you are too. What makes you a god if you can die like any other man?"

"Protecting my people is what makes me a god," he replied. "Instead, you want me to send them into a situation where you can't guarantee their safety. You have no idea what we're walking into."

Of course, he was right.

Pax's vision of the future haunted me. "We can resolve this peacefully. We *will* resolve this peacefully. We have to." *If I can't use his ego against him, maybe I can exploit his self-interest.* "Besides, what if the Terrans find out about you? That there's an artilect, the very thing they helped destroy the world to prevent, living a few miles away. What would you do then? Flee to draw any conflict away from your followers? Or expect them to die defending you?"

"That would never happen. No one knows about us," he said, but the paleness of his face told me otherwise.

"I'm sure my tolerance for torture wouldn't be very high, Oliver. I'd probably tell them everything I knew."

"Maybe you'd never get that far. It's a dangerous world out there."

Tor stiffened next to me, and I brushed his arm. "We'd expose you long before that ever happened. These people are resourceful. They'd survive."

"Oliver, after this, you can come back here. You don't have to stay with us." Tor tried to placate him.

"Thank you, Tor. How very magnanimous of you."

"Can we please come up with a plan? We can fight about this later." *We don't have time for this.*

After an hour, we'd finally devised a strategy. I wasn't sure it was the best, but it was the only one we agreed on. Tor and I were to go on ahead, while Oliver got the Saints of Loving Grace organized. We would act as scouts, reporting back to Oliver when they arrived.

I sketched a rough map for them to follow, trying to be as specific as possible.

Oliver barely glanced at it. "You don't know where they are, do you?"

"I do. It's… We haven't *been* there, as such."

163

By this time, Oliver was herding us toward the door. "Whatever. We'll manage."

"And remember, nobody gets hurt!" We had to avoid Pax's future, or we were done for, all of us.

"Oh, for fuck's sake. This is a brilliant plan, isn't it? Who cares if a few Terrans get wounded? They're obsolete."

"Yes, well, you've got no choice now, do you?"

"You're wrong, Ailith. There's always a choice." And with that, he slammed the door in our faces.

"...and with assassination of Novus CEO Robin Leung, the Prime Minister has called for an indefinite ban on further research and production of any artificial life. Those still in existence will be allowed to live out their natural lives—if you can call it that—but all individuals with robotic components have been issued with a notice of removal. That goes for anything functional or cosmetic. Now, we've heard rumors of cyborgs who don't have any noticeable physical differences, who appear to be fully organic, but these rumors are unsubstantiated and likely started by those who wish to stir up further controversy..."

—Shirley Novak, CNN Tech Watch, 2040

35
KALBIR

I had to admit; Ahar was stunning. Red had always made me look sallow, but the crimson fabric of her lehenga choli made her skin look like tawny cream. Our mother had spent months on the intricate embroidery, coaxing peacocks and twisting vines out of the gold satin. She had pricked her fingers many times while sewing it; I hoped the blood-spotted ribbons would prove to be a blessing.

Our mother was annoyed because I, the eldest sister, showed zero interest in getting married. I'd tried to explain it to her on numerous occasions, but she simply pursed her lips and turned away. Ahar understood. She knew I wanted more than the future our mother wanted for me. I'd wanted more from the time I was a little girl.

Mother, of course, would argue, saying I would still be able to do everything I wanted, that I could have a husband, and children, and the career I'd always dreamed of. But I couldn't, and Ahar knew it. She'd kept my secret, even from Aadi, and would keep it until my death, if that should happen.

Ahar turned slightly, catching my eye and smiling. To me, she seemed stifled, weighed down by the heavy gold of her jewelry. The red and ivory of the bangles I'd given her this morning reflected the overhead light. She'd placed them above all the others on her arm, closest to her heart.

My ass was aching as the Giani began the prayers of the laavan pheras. I surreptitiously checked my watch: it had already been half an hour. I shifted, trying to relieve the pressure. The bottom of my choli cut into my stomach.

Why had I eaten so much?

The fullness of my belly lulled me; my eyelids drooped. I stifled a laugh, picturing my mother's face if I were to fall asleep. She was already annoyed with me. I'd wanted to wear black today—it was the color I was most comfortable in. We'd fought, and now I was wearing green.

My attention wandered from the ceremony to the gurudwara itself. The ornate white columns and arches of the temple soared over the crowd, inlaid with colorful enamel flowers and leaves and festooned with massive ivory peonies and orchids. Had they been carved by human hands? Or had they come off some robotic assembly line? My heart quailed.

I was entering the Pantheon Modern cyborg program in a few days. Would I become a robot? Mindless, capable of only performing specific mundane tasks, over and over? Would that be any different from my life now?

No. They'd assured me I would still be the same person, just better. Besides, whatever was going to happen, it had to be better than being ordinary.

Even so, Ahar couldn't understand why I would want to become a cyborg. When I'd gone to her with the news of my acceptance, she'd bustled me into her closet and shut the door the way she'd done when we were children.

"Aren't you worried about what's going to happen to you afterward? If people will still see you as human? What if they treat you the way they treat the robots?" she'd whispered as we'd crouched in the dark.

She had a point. Robots weren't exactly treated well right now with all the tension between the Cosmists and the Terrans. I'd seen many of them being abused, ignored, spat on…even knocked over in the street as they minded their own business.

It was especially hard for the androids, the ones who looked so human. I'd have thought creating them to mimic us would make people want to protect them, to treat them with kindness, but it seemed to have the opposite effect. The more human they seemed, the more people wanted to exploit them.

Cyborgs were a little different. For some people, like those who'd lost limbs, it made sense. And it was fashionable in some circles. Dermal augmentations were popular with the kids in our neighborhood, the incandescent patterns flashing and throbbing under their skin. But those were teenagers, and the implants were temporary. Choosing to become a cyborg when you didn't have to, making a machine a permanent part of yourself, was a different matter altogether. And everybody, Terrans and Cosmists alike, agreed on that.

"Ahar! Relax. They've assured me that nobody will be able to tell I'm a cyborg. I'll look completely human. Anyway, I don't care. I want people to know. It's their problem if they can't accept it."

"That's hardly helped the androids, though, has it? Seriously Kal, for all your open-mindedness about robots and cyborgs, not once have I ever heard you defend them when someone we know has spoken against them, or worse. You just like to talk about how liberal you are. You still look the other way."

It hurt because it was true. "Well, I'm making up for it now, aren't I?"

"Plus, what will Mother say? What will her friends say?" Ahar tried to look severe, but the thought of our mother's best friend, Mrs. Kahttri's, face was too much and she snorted. I hadn't dared to tell Mother what I'd been up to. Although she would never openly discriminate against a cyborg or even a robot, she was staunchly on the Terran side of the artilect debate. She didn't mind cyborgs as much, since she saw them as humans with some machine parts, but the most recent android models made her nervous. I had to admit, they seemed pretty damn close to human, talking and smiling stiffly as they went about their duties, but it wasn't like they were sentient. They were glorified toasters.

She'd whispered to my aunty that she didn't mind the androids per se, since they were useful, and did my aunty know that Mrs. Khattri had one? And it did all the work at home and made wonderful roti, and wasn't that incredible, but why did they have to make them appear so human? Why give them faces and eight fingers and two thumbs, two arms and two legs? My aunty had wondered if Mrs. Khattri's android was anatomically correct, scandalizing my mother.

There was a man standing by one of the pillars, just out of sight of the general crowd. He looked straight out of television: tall and broad, his silver hair shorn close to his skull. He wore pressed black trousers and a black button-up shirt. A tinted visor obscured his eyes.

I glanced around. No one else seemed to notice him. But he noticed me. He held up a black card, with a single bronze symbol embossed on it. I had to squint to make it out.

A stylized PM. Pantheon Modern. Crap. Where the hell was my mother? Whatever he wanted, it couldn't be good.

Voices rose in chorus to the final hymns, and my attention snapped back to the wedding. It was nearly over. I had to get that man out of view before my mother saw him and wandered over to welcome him, throwing her arms around him like he was just another member of the family.

As the karah parshad was passed around, Ahar smiled at me.

168

She truly did look radiant. Aadi, his fingers resting on the hilt of his *krijpan*, winked at me. She was going to tell him tonight that she was pregnant. He'd be overjoyed. An unexpected pang of sadness caught me off guard.

As the guests filed out of the temple, the stranger's hand fell on my shoulder. "Kalbir Anand?"

"Yes."

"My name is Dominic. We need to talk."

"Fine, but not here. Follow me." I kept my eyes on my mother. She was busy accepting congratulations and hadn't noticed us yet. We mingled with the crowd until we reached the main hallway. I pulled him down to the end, where there was an alcove just large enough for the two of us and a hideous orange vase.

"What's going on?"

"I'm from Pantheon Modern."

"Yeah, I can see that. What do you want? Why are you here? This isn't really a good time."

"It never is," he replied. "We have a problem."

"What do you mean? What problem?"

Did they find out I'd told Ahar everything? Was I in trouble?

"Look, I—"

"Program Omega has been compromised." Even though his voice was low, I peeked around the corner to see if anyone was listening. The hall had fallen silent. Everyone was getting into their cars to head to the reception hall.

"What does that mean? I'm no longer a part of it?"

"That's up to you. Things are going to start moving very fast now. If you want to remain part of the program, you have to come with me, now."

"Now? I can't come now. My sister just got married. People will notice if I'm not there."

"It doesn't matter."

"You've never met my mother."

"People will be looking for you. To kill you."

169

"What? But I'm not even a cyborg yet!"

"It doesn't matter. You will be."

"Fine. Then I won't go through with it. I won't tell anyone anything."

"No, you won't." He opened his blazer. A tiny syringe was tucked into his waistband. He shifted his weight, trapping me in the alcove.

Cold realization dawned.

"I'm sorry," he said.

"Wait. Stop, please."

"Miss Anand, I came here to help you. I don't think you understand the stakes here. I can't let you go. You may think you can keep a secret, but you can't."

"I—" *I wanted to insist that I could, but he was right. I hadn't kept it a secret from Ahar.*

Ahar. Did they know I'd told her?

"So my only choice is to come with you now, or you'll kill me?"

"Yes. I can only protect you if you come with me. If I can't protect you, I have to kill you. A war has started, Miss Anand, and you're part of it, whether you like it or not. What part of it you are is up to you."

Tears blurred my vision. I bit my lip to try to stop them.

Dominic laid his hand on my arm. "Please, miss. I don't want to kill you. I'm trying to save you. I... You've been my charge from the beginning. I don't want to lose you." *He removed the visor. He was younger than I'd first suspected, prematurely gray. His eyes matched my choli, the vibrant green of old jade.*

"You've been following me since the beginning? That was months ago."

"Yes. Please, let me take you with me."

"How do I know you're not one of the people who want to kill me?"

"You don't. You have to trust me."

My mother. Ahar. What would they do if I suddenly

170

disappeared? It would kill my mother, ruin the start of Ahar's marriage.

My death, right here and now, would be worse. Wouldn't it?

"If you've been following me for so long, then you know my mother, my sister?"

"Yes."

"If I disappear… They… Please, can I have until tomorrow? Ahar leaves for her honeymoon. I'll think of something to tell my mother. That I need to go away for work or something. Please?"

He didn't say anything for what seemed like hours. A car horn honked outside. Mother.

It seemed to rouse him. "Fine. Tomorrow. Talk to no one until then. I'll be watching. If I have to take you out, I will."

I crashed through the front doors of the hall just as my mother was reaching them.

"Kalbir! There you are. Where have you—" She saw the tearstains on my face and patted my arm. "Oh, foolish girl. Don't you worry. You'll see just as much of Ahar as before. They only live around the corner."

I hiccupped. "I know. It's just that I'll miss her. Things will be different now. Everything's changing."

"Things must change, or the world will stop turning. You'll be sisters forever, no matter what happens."

As we drove away from the gurudwara, I wondered just how long forever would be.

"…Actually, Shirley, you wouldn't even need nuclear weapons to destroy the world. Nothing as brutal as that. You get enough cities burning for long enough at the right time of year, and boom, total disruption to the ecosystem. Wildfires and incendiary lightning would wipe out arable land. Smoke would fill the clouds, and toxic rain would fall. Not to mention how people would react. You've seen how they get when they think they're going to be snowed in for a few days…"

—*Alexander Petrov, CNN Tech Watch, 2040*

36

AILITH

"Do you think they'll show up?" We had stopped to rest, and I'd followed one of the glittering threads. The fullness in my belly from food I hadn't eaten was strangely comforting.

"I'm not sure. I don't think you should've threatened him like that. He's not the kind of man to take something like that lightly."

I didn't want to admit it, but I agreed. The expression on Oliver's face as he'd shut the door promised murder. *I don't care.* We'd deal with Oliver after Pax and Cindra were safe.

We'd walked through the night and most of the morning to reach the area of the Terran camp. It had been a miserable trek.

The mountain pass was freezing, a harsh coldness that

was agonizing to breathe. Flanked by miles of sheer rock face on one side and near-vertical embankment on the other, we'd been forced to take the road. The asphalt was marred with potholes and long, vicious cracks, the painted lines weathered away.

Avalanches had strewn sections of our path with debris, and we picked our way around the chunks of stone swiftly and silently, straining our ears for the telltale rumble. At the crest of the pass was a wide shoulder where tourists could pull over and view the forest in all its immense splendor. To me, it looked like an instrument of torture, infinite metal spikes waiting for a curious misstep.

By the time we'd crossed and were picking our way down the other side, my lungs felt as though they'd collapse.

"You'd think they would've given us reinforced lungs." Each word felt like it would be my last.

Tor's laugh was barely more than a wheeze. "They were probably worried we'd make smoking a thing again."

"Ailith? Are you here?"

Pax. I was finally going to be able to tell him yes.

We could see the windmill now, cobbled together from stone and what appeared to be metal grating. It spun idly. The wind that had taken our breath away in the pass had little power here.

The connection between us was clear, and I pinpointed their location.

"Yes! Pax, we're here. Well, almost. We're about a mile away."

"Good. Is Oliver with you?"

"Not yet, but he's coming. And he's leading reinforcements."

Pax's relief swept through me, a flurry that warmed my chest. *"Something's happening. I think we're out of time."*

"What? What do you mean, Pax? What's happening?"

"The ones who insisted on using the nanites, they're dying. I believe

173

they're going to kill us."

"Don't worry. We won't let them hurt you. Tell Cindra we're coming."

"And Oliver is coming, for sure?"

"Yes," I lied. *"He'll be here any minute."* I hope.

At the outskirts of the Terran village, an irregular wood-and-wire fence wove in and out of the trees, knotted scraps of cloth swaying in the mild wind. It was strangely still. No guards patrolled the perimeter; nobody was watching out for strangers.

"I can't see anyone."

Tor's face drew tight. "Yeah, I noticed that too. Believe me, it's not a good thing."

"What do you mean? Is it not just carelessness?"

"It could mean they believe they're too strong to fear outsiders. They have five years of experience surviving, so their confidence is probably justified. Or, like Pax said, something is happening, something important. It may also mean they've seen us, and they want us to think they haven't. They might've been aware of us all along." He put his hand on my arm. "Ailith, I know you don't want to hear this, but you have to consider the possibility that Pax has told them about us."

"He wouldn't! He…" Pax's unnatural calmness. His insistence that Oliver be with us. *Could it be that he…?* "No. I don't think it's possible." I didn't sound convincing even to my own ears. "But Cindra…what I saw…what she felt—"

"He may not have intended to betray you, Ailith. But if they're being tortured…they've been captive for days. And people have no law but their own moral compass now. If you were a Terran, you would believe in the rightness of what they were doing, no matter how extreme the method."

"I would never torture someone! I don't even want the Terrans to get hurt. Even if they are monsters." The fuse on my temper started to burn.

"I'm not saying what they're doing is right. But you've only been awake for a couple of weeks. These people have lived in this world for *five years*. They didn't survive through kindness."

"You don't know that!" I didn't want him to be right. Pax's vision of the future hovered at the edge of my mind.

"Look, I hope you're right." He squeezed my hand. "Ailith, despite what these people have done, we can't let them be hurt. We were supposed to act as a bridge between the Cosmists and the Terrans. Nothing's changed. If we play it right, maybe they'll let go of the past and work together. I mean, none of that matters anymore, does it? Nobody's going to be creating artilects now. The war is over. They need to help each other. You've seen what will happen otherwise."

"I agree with you on that, at least," I replied.

We found a copse on a rise close to the camp that would allow us to observe it while keeping out of sight. Not that it mattered. Either the Terrans had already seen us, or they were too distracted to notice. We finally had the opportunity to see the people who were capable of committing such terrible acts against other human beings.

I wasn't sure what I'd expected evil to look like, but I was disappointed. The Terran village seemed like any other village before the war, albeit more rustic. The houses were similar to those of the Saints, though clad in patched, modern, slatted siding rather than metal sheets. Behind them, the backyards were open, strewn with the debris of normal lives.

The few children I saw were bundled up against the cold, darting from house to house as they chased each other. Teenagers gathered sticks, which they threw onto a growing pile. Women and men alike were busy with a slew of mundane activities. Some were hanging plants for drying, others, meat. Laughter wafted on the air, mingled with the smells of cooking.

If I hadn't seen them electrocuting Cindra with my own eyes, felt it on our skin, I never would've believed it.

"How many people do you think there are?" I asked Tor.

He scanned the village. "I'm not sure. Eighty, maybe ninety. There may be even more inside."

Ninety people. Less than half the number of the Saints. I liked those odds.

"They look so normal," I said.

A sad smile tugged at the corners of Tor's mouth. "What did you expect? Evil comes in all forms. It's a matter of perspective."

I was about to argue with him that, no, torturing innocent people was *not* a matter of perspective when there was a stirring below us. Whatever Pax had predicted was going to happen was happening *now*. And Oliver was nowhere in sight.

Word passed quickly and quietly through the crowd. Terrans gathered at the north end of the village, where two thick poles stood. A commotion from the south drew our attention. *Pax and Cindra.* For the first time, I saw them from the outside. They looked different through my own eyes.

The Terrans hadn't bothered to dress them for the cold. Cindra was stumbling, long hair matted over her face. Her bronze skin was marred with burns, and the scars of many others were fading on her thin arms. It made me ill, knowing how quickly we healed. Those marks weren't torture for information, but for pleasure.

176

Pax walked calmly, head up, eyes searching for me.

"No one's coming to help you, freak," someone jeered.

That was some good news, at least; they didn't know we were here. One of the men flanking Pax punched him in the back of the head. As he fell to his knees, I gently pulled on his thread.

"Pax! Stop looking for us. You'll give us away."

"Is Oliver here?"

"No, not yet."

"He must be here!"

"He'll be here, I promise. You'll understand when you meet him. He likes to make a grand entrance." I hoped it was a promise I would keep. *Come on, Oliver, you asshole.*

The Terrans led Pax and Cindra to the two poles and began tying each to one.

"Scared yet?" one of the men asked Pax.

Pax seemed to consider the question for a few seconds then shook his head. The man slipped a knife from under his coat and slid it between Pax's ribs. He grunted and doubled over, but didn't cry out. The man angled the knife for another thrust.

"I've had enough. Forget waiting for Oliver. I'm not going to sit here and watch Pax get stabbed to death." I started to stand.

"Ailith, stop." Tor's voice was cold steel.

"Tor, we have to help him. We can't—"

"He'll heal. We have to give Oliver more time."

"What if he doesn't come?" We were both thinking it.

Tor ignored me. "We still have some time. Wait."

Every nerve in my body was pulled taut as the Terrans finished tying Pax and Cindra to the poles and piled up wood around their feet. They were going to burn them alive.

"Tor."

"Not many other ways to kill a cyborg." The muscles in his jaw worked overtime. He was getting close to his limit. Had Pax seen what I had? The others like us, immolating themselves? Had he told the Terrans? Or was it a lucky guess?

A heated discussion broke out within the crowd beneath us.

"I can't believe you're actually going to go through with this. I though you merely wanted to scare them. *We* can't do this."

The speaker was one of the women I'd seen hanging herbs.

"They've not done anything."

"Not done anything? They've killed us, Naomi. Cole, Seska—they're dead because of these two."

"They *told* you the nanites wouldn't work on us. They told you it would kill them. You didn't want to listen."

The man ignored her "They're abominations, anyway. If it weren't for their kind, we wouldn't be here, living like this. Like savages. I was a fucking architect before their war."

"It wasn't just *their* war. And abomination?" she scoffed. "You were perfectly happy to take advantage of their *abomination* when you thought it would help you. When we found each other, when we established this camp, we agreed there would be no more unnecessary violence. How else are we supposed to survive?"

"They're not human." He said it slowly, as though he were speaking to a child. "How many times can we have this discussion? Does that seem human to you?" He pointed at Pax, who was standing straight again, his wounds forgotten.

"Of course they are. Look at them!"

"I am. This is how they get you. Why do you think they

changed them only on the inside? Why do you think the Cosmists wanted to make artilects look human? They will invade us quietly, like a cancer, destroying us one by one until we're extinct. How can you be so blind?"

"Who's *they*? There is no 'they.' They're not *artilects*! They're human. So what if they've been…enhanced? We should be working *with* them, using their abilities to help us survive."

Murmurs of assent passed between some members of the crowd, but none spoke up for us.

"Anyone else who thinks we should let them live, step forward. Let them murder us in our sleep. Enslave our children."

"Oh Jack, for God's—"

"Who else?" he thundered. The crowd was silent. "Right. It's decided. Let's get on with it. I want to have this ugly business finished. Now."

Oliver, where are you?

"Can't you see into Oliver?" Tor asked. "Find out where they are?"

"Yes. No. I can't. I need to be here if something happens. I might not be able to get out of him in time."

The woman, Naomi, stepped back into the crowd, her face ashen. Jack and another man lit two large torches and approached the poles. Cindra screamed. Pax remained as calm as ever.

"Tor?" I gathered myself into a crouch.

Jack bent to place the torch at Cindra's feet. Naomi shouted and tried to push her way to the stakes. While some people strove to hold her back, reality set in for others, and they began pushing through the crowd.

A roar sounded behind us. Oliver had arrived. But that wasn't right. We were supposed to go in quietly, diplomatically, our hands raised in peace.

179

The Saints rushed past us; they were armed.
That future was happening, now.

We believed we would know our Divine when we saw him. How could we not? Not only would he emerge from the maelstrom unscathed while the rest of the world was branded by the fire, but he would bring the dead back to life, sort the righteous from the unbelievers, and lead us forward into a new future.

—Celeste Steed, *The Second Coming*

37
AILITH

"You'll regret this."

I should've paid attention.

Someone once told me that when something terrible happened, time slowed. I wished that was true. I could've stopped what was happening. But it didn't, and I couldn't.

Oliver and his followers swarmed into the Terran camp and cut them down. They wore their martyrdom on their faces, their destiny finally coming to pass. Oliver gazed up to where Tor and I were still crouched in shock and smirked his triumph.

There's always a choice.

The Saints didn't discriminate as they killed. Axes rose and fell, metal grated against bone, and precious bullets shrieked from the mouths of rifles. The air became hazy, and the ground finally got the moisture it so desperately needed.

Celeste reigned in the middle of the fray, her hair

braided on top of her head like some warrior of old. Her lips were drawn back in a primal scream, and blood smeared her teeth. The Terrans scrambled for whatever weapons they could lay their hands on and tried to fight back.

From the pain in my throat, I was shouting, but the sound was drowned out by the furor below. Pax and Cindra were still tied to their posts, vulnerable and forgotten. The future Pax had shown me was supposed to be a distant one, not today. Darkness bloomed behind my eyes.

No. No. this can't be happening. I have to stop this.

I sprinted down the hill and entered the churning mass, grabbing the woman called Naomi from behind. I needed to make her stop, help her see reason. If anyone would listen to me, she would.

Her shoulders and her collarbone crushed and splintered beneath my hands. *My hands.* They were too large, too strong.

Tor's hands.

She tried to turn toward me, but I held her fast. My hands wouldn't let go. The jagged ends of her collarbone had punctured her neck, and she was bleeding.

Too much. Too fast.

When I finally released her, it was too late. As she fell to the ground at my feet, something in me that had been stretched too thin finally broke. I didn't want to hurt anyone, but I could no longer stop myself.

I seized the body closest to me. Saint or Terran, I didn't care; I just wanted them to stop. To be still. But the strength of Tor's body was out of my control. He'd had five years to learn restraint. I had seconds. Skin tore beneath my hands. Muscles ripped away from bone. Bullets peppered my chest, and still, I couldn't stop.

182

Finally, someone managed to slice the tendons in my legs and I fell facedown onto the sodden earth. A sudden rush, a painful tearing in my mind, and I was back on the hill, on my back above the battlefield.

Tor lay motionless below; Pax stood above him, holding an axe slick with blood. Someone must've cut him free. I charged down the hill and barreled into him, crushing the breath out of his lanky body.

"You! You've betrayed us." I closed my hands around his throat.

"No. It was the only way to stop you," he said, his voice low and soothing. "It's over. Look."

I wanted to believe him. Tightening my hands around his neck, I risked an upward glance. He was right; it was over.

The ground was littered with bodies. Not a single Terran had been spared. Taken by surprise, they hadn't made sense of the chaos in time to fight back. Of the Saints of Loving Grace, nearly all were still standing. Celeste stood amongst the survivors, her face rosy with victory. She caught my eye and winked conspiratorially.

Dead. So many people. Dead. All because of me.

This time, I didn't vomit.

Tor.

I released Pax and dropped to his side. The gaping wounds in his calves flaunted bone, though the flesh had begun to knit together. It took all my strength to turn him over. He was a mess. Blood leaked from the slowly closing wounds in his chest. The bullets, pushed to the surface by the nanites, seemed far too small to cause such damage. His face was pale, his eyes closed.

I leaned forward to whisper in his ear. I wanted to tell him how sorry I was, how I hadn't meant for this, *any* of this, to happen.

183

As he felt my breath on his face, his hand shot out and gripped my arm. "Don't. Don't touch me. Never touch me again." His words were a splinter in my heart.

"Tor, I'm sorry. I'm so, so sorry." His fingers on my arm were agony, but I didn't pull away. "Tor, please."

"Go. Away."

"Well, that was fun, wasn't it?" Oliver swaggered over to where Tor lay, not a mark on him. "So much for your 'let's-all-love-each-other' plan."

"You did this." This kind of rage was new to me, and not unwelcome.

I'll kill him. Why not? I've had some practice today.

The voice inside me whooped. As I struggled to my feet, Tor's body twitched, and the blackness swirled at the edge of my vision.

No. No. No!

I was thrust back into myself by Celeste's scream. She was pointing at Tor, upset because he was injured.

But not for his sake.

"Blood. He's *bleeding*."

I didn't understand until I saw Oliver's face, horrified and frozen.

We'd been outed. Artilects didn't bleed.

We were in trouble.

"...and that's just in the short-term. Eventually that smoke would generate an ash cloud substantial enough to block the sun. And the effects would last for years. Freezing temperatures, very little sunlight, reduced precipitation, a thinning ozone. Nothing could survive. Not plants, not animals, not people. That's it. The human race is extinct. Yes, some would survive initially. But without food, potable water, or medical attention, for how long?"

—Alexander Petrov, CNN Tech Watch, 2040

38

AILITH

The air was as crisp as always when we arrived at the market. I waved at the other farmers as my father wove through the barricades to our regular stall. People were already lined up down the block; only the steel fences kept them from swarming us and fighting each other tooth and nail for a misshapen carrot. Well, that and the armed guards.

Who would've supposed vegetables would one day be worth more than their weight in gold? Not my father, that was for sure. When he was young, farmers were overlooked and under-valued. Now, thanks to a few mistakes with genetics and changes in the political climate, farmers were like rock stars.

We hadn't had a food shortage, far from it. But the sheer exclusivity of food grown in the ground was enough to make the most pest-riddled cauliflower a prize. Our specialty was garlic. Gourmet garlic grown from heirloom strains hundreds of years old; we were one of the few places left in the province licensed to grow it.

It was go-time. As soon as people were let through the gate, a crowd gathered in front of our stall. I lifted the bulb of garlic where they could see it. It was the first of the season, its picturesque skin a satiny-white mottled with silky purple, clinging tightly and softly undulating over each clove.

I slid the outer wrapper off with my thumb, careful not to press too hard and damage the flesh. The outer skin came off easily, the second, third, and fourth were progressively tighter. I took my time, but this close to the prize, the crowd was impatient, and the process was almost painful.

I broke the skin around the top of the bulb with my thumb, and the spiked tips of the cloves poked through. My thumb slid down either side of a single clove and broke it free from the cluster. It was firm and plump, encased in a dusky rose-colored skin, streaked with a rich walnut brown. The faintest scent rose from the plate at the bottom. Saliva rushed into my mouth, and the crowd before me licked their lips.

I sliced the end off the clove I'd liberated, the pungent tang stinging the inside of my nose. I inhaled deeply, and the crowd mimicked me, sighing in anticipation as I peeled off the rest of the skin. The cream-colored clove was smooth and round. Perfect.

I cut a thin slice and held it up to the crowd. It glistened wetly, my fingers sticky from its oil. I placed it on the tongue of the woman directly in front of me and watched as the raw garlic stung her mouth. She exhaled slowly through her nose, the scorching oil dripping down her throat.

My dad grinned at me. He would miss me being here with him. His natural shyness made him an awkward showman. Selling the garlic wasn't my thing either—I much preferred the growing—but since the death of my younger brother and mother last year, we'd needed each other to keep going. Selling had been my mother's job. She'd been the reason our stall was so popular, her small hands making the bulbs appear huge as she held them aloft with a delicate

186

flourish, her voice so soft and rhythmic it caused the hairs on the back of your neck to stand up as you leaned in to catch every word.

A commotion a few stalls down the street caught the attention of the crowd. Guards pushed people back to form a perimeter around a package on the ground. More and more of these parcels had appeared lately. The police never said who the targets were, and nobody ever claimed responsibility. Everyone had a theory, of course. Some believed it was the Terrans protesting the development of AI, others that it was the Cosmists trying to demonstrate how necessary their technology was.

The guards forced through the whispering crowd, a bomb-disposal robot in tow. One of them typed instructions into the keypad on its back then it lay down and enveloped the bomb with its body. The crowd hushed and waited. At the last moment, before the bomb exploded, the robot turned its head in my direction. It had no eyes — they hadn't wanted to upset people by blowing up robots that were too humanoid—but it was looking at me.

The device finally obliged the crowd and exploded, the bot's body expanding slightly as it absorbed the impact. As the police dragged the ruined bot away, the crowd muttered in disappointment at the anti-climax.

"It doesn't seem fair, does it?" I said.

"What do you mean?" my father asked. He was inspecting the spot where the robot had lain.

"Using them like that. I mean, that's it. It's dead."

His jaw tensed. This was not a subject he liked to talk about. He'd become resolutely Terran after my mother and brother had died. He blamed robots and those who created them for their deaths, though it had been an accident. No one knew exactly why hundreds of automated vehicles had simply driven off the road. My father blamed the manufacturer, Novus, even though there was no evidence they were at fault. Only rumors.

"They're not alive, Ailith. Just because something looks, walks, and acts like a person, doesn't mean it is."

187

"I know, but still. Doesn't it seem a bit cruel to you? To build them simply for the purpose of killing them?"

"Would you rather it had been a person covering that bomb? Getting themselves blown to bits?"

"Of course not. I'd rather there weren't bombs in the first place."

His mouth pressed into a thin line. We'd had this conversation before, and the outcome was always the same: us feeling awkward around each other for the rest of the day. He didn't understand why the Cosmists wanted to create artilects, why they wanted to create new life when there was already so much around them.

"Why can't they have children?" he'd say. He was even less comfortable with cyborgs. "It's unnatural. They're making themselves less human."

Since I'd become ill, he no longer said that. Though he hated the idea of cyborgs, in my case, he at least understood the attraction. My body was failing. Tomorrow, I was going to the hospital for what might be the last time. They couldn't cure what I had; slowing it down was the best they could do. But my doctor had called yesterday, with a new option. Something to do with nanites. He didn't have time to explain the details to me. And although my father didn't agree, he loved me.

He would understand. Even if I had tiny machines running through my veins, I'd still be me.

Omega, for you to understand how you're here, in this place, I must start at the beginning. Much of what I'll say, you won't understand. Many of these words, these ideas, will mean nothing to you, but they were meaningful to us, and it's because of us that you are here.

—*Cindra, Letter to Omega*

39

AILITH

We were back at the Saints of Loving Grace village. I'd tried to comfort myself by briefly living someone else's life, but I'd found only my own memories instead. It was strange being yourself inside yourself.

The Saints had called us the 'Children of Perdition,' and we were in no shape to insist otherwise. I had no idea what that even meant. We should've run; the Saints were no match for our speed or stamina. But we couldn't. Cindra was in shock. Tor was still injured. Oliver believed he could ingratiate himself with his followers again, and Pax, he continued as normal, as though we were simply on a day out from the asylum.

I could've run, gotten away, and come back for them later. But I couldn't leave them, especially Tor. After what had happened, and with whatever was going to happen, we needed to stick together. I'd caused this, and I would get us out of it.

They eventually put us in a horse shelter encased with

electrified wire, as though we were some kind of exhibit. Which, I guessed, we were. The village had sacrificed their house lights to supply its power. Trying to suck up, Oliver had tipped them off about the mechanical parts of us being vulnerable to electric shock. It wouldn't kill us, but it would incapacitate us. They'd forced us in with an axe to Cindra's throat. I bet Oliver had told them how useful beheading was as well. *Fucking Oliver.* He was the gift that kept on giving.

They called a meeting in the hall to decide what would become of us. A scuffle broke out at the door, as the men of the camp filed in and tried to shut it behind them. It was clear those days were over. A sizable group of women, led by Celeste and still wielding their weapons from the slaughter, forced their way in. The door slammed shut, and a few minutes later, half the men came back out, their faces subdued.

Oliver sulked in a front corner by himself, waiting for one of his former worshippers to acknowledge him. He caught me watching him and curled his lip. "Happy, Ailith? They're probably going to kill us now."

"Why did you do it, Oliver? How did you ever think it would end well?"

"I told you you'd regret coming here," he replied softly.

"That's how you planned to make me regret it? By killing a bunch of innocent people?"

Oliver laughed. "They weren't *innocent*. Surviving a war doesn't make someone innocent. Those people you killed are the same ones who would've prevented your existence in the first place if they'd had a choice. Think about what they were going to do. Murder two people just because their intention to exploit them wasn't paying off."

He dug the toe of his boot into the dirt floor. "They've been scavenging weapons and survivors, gathering their strength. What do you think they would've done if they'd discovered the Saints of Loving Grace?" he asked, gesturing toward the surrounding village. "Do you really think they would've let us live in peace?"

"Your false peace. You *lied* to these people, Oliver," I reminded him.

Wait.

"Gathering their strength? You knew about the Terrans, didn't you? You used us."

He examined his fingernails. "Yes, I did. I make things that threaten us my business. Your friend there would've done the same." He inclined his head toward Tor, where he slumped against the wall. "I would've come up with other means to deal with them, but you forced my hand."

"Other means? Like what? Cutting their heads off while they were defenseless? We went to your bunker. We saw what you did."

He crossed his arms over his chest. "I did what I had to do. She was a threat to us, to you. Again, your friend would've done the same thing."

"No, he wouldn't. He's not a murderer."

Oliver laughed at that. "Well, if he wasn't before, he is now, thanks to you." His words were a sucker punch to my gut. It hurt all the more because he was right. Whether I'd meant to or not, I'd soaked Tor's hands with blood.

"You've ruined everything. You should've let me be. Look what you've done to these people. You've changed them forever, made them idolaters. Generations of sacrifice and preparation, for nothing. God doesn't exist for them anymore."

He's right.

The previous tranquility and bustling cheerfulness of the Saints was gone. People clustered together in small groups, their voices low. Amid their whispers, some

191

watched us. The rest watched each other.

"Me? Oliver, *you're* the one who told them you were a god. How long did you think it would last? They'd have found out eventually. And what would you have done then? Slaughtered them all and moved on?"

He was saved from answering by Celeste. Her hair was still knotted on her head, her face painted with blood. She stood taller, her former meekness gone.

"Celeste." The relief in Oliver's voice was clear. "You've come. I—"

"You've been sentenced to death," she said flatly, studying his face.

"Celeste! Why are you doing this? I thought we—"

"We what? Had something? Everything we had was based on a lie, Oliver. And not merely a lie. You've made us unbelievers, followers of a false god. You took our faith and twisted it, perverted it. You've condemned us all to Hell on this earth. Do you know they want me to die along with you? Because of what you did to me?"

"Condemned you? Did it ever occur to you that this might actually *be* Hell? And what I did *to* you? Are you sure you're not pissed because you found out you weren't spreading it for some machine? It's not like you needed much convincing." His lips twisted.

"They're not going to kill you, are they?" I interrupted. Even with everything that was happening, I didn't want Celeste to pay for what we'd done. The Saints massacre of the Terrans was reprehensible, but it had happened because of us. We'd manipulated them and exploited their faith and fear; the blame was ours.

"No." Celeste leaned forward on the handle of her axe. "Did you know that Oliver told us it was a Terran *military* camp, filled only with fighting men and women? That we went in willing to kill and die for your glorious cause?"

I stared at Oliver, incredulous. "No, I didn't."

Celeste continued. "See, one good thing that came from being manipulated into butchering other defenseless women and children is that we can never go back. We're no longer defenseless." She shifted her gaze to me. "It's a shame we need to kill *you*, Ailith. I understand you only did what you felt was right, like we did. You, on the other hand," she said, turning back to Oliver, "did not."

She leaned away from us and snapped her fingers at our guard. "Turn off the power."

He hesitated.

"Turn it off!" she snarled, fingering the blade of her axe.

As the humming of the bars went silent, Celeste sidled up to Oliver. "I suppose I should thank you," she said. "If you hadn't betrayed us, we'd still be living in the dark, waiting for a savior who was never going to come. Allowing our bodies to belong to anyone but ourselves, because we'd been told it was the right way, the way it's always been. But you've opened our eyes. Now we're going to save ourselves. You see," she said, low enough that only Oliver and I heard, "your deaths are only the beginning." She traced her hand down the side of Oliver's face and over his chest.

"What about all the pleasure I gave you?" Oliver whispered as she ran her fingers over the front of his trousers. She cupped him, and he let out a small gasp.

"Oh, sweetie," she replied with a sympathetic smile. "My pleasure was about as real as you were. Turn it back on." She gave me one last nod before walking away.

The swinging of her hips faded as another thread pulled me down.

"...all the fledging cyborgs have increased physical strength, although this has been concentrated in some more than others. Some have had emotional adjustments to make them more prone to certain reactions and decision-making methods. Memory capabilities and computational processes are also increased, but because the enhancements work differently in each subject we have no idea which will take, and if taken, to what degree. And as hard as we try to select applicants that are both physically and mentally capable of surviving the cyberization process, as you can see from our current rates, survival remains our biggest challenge. Causes of death vary, but most commonly include immune rejection of the nanites, heart attack, and, rarely, consumption by the nanites themselves. And then there are those who cannot cope psychologically with the changes, who become lost and aren't able to find their way back..."

—*Mil Cothi, Pantheon Modern Cyborg Program Omega, 2040*

40
KALBIR

I was the one to find Ros and Adrian on their knees, their hands entwined. Cowards.

Though they weren't really. It took a lot of balls to burn yourself alive, and more to be still and quiet while you're doing it. I gave them that, at least.

In hindsight, I'd seen it coming. The last few days they'd been too *calm. They'd seemed to be coming to terms with everything and finally adapting, but no. They must've been planning it all along.*

Lexa had relaxed enough to stop standing guard in the hallway. Besides the practical loss of their abilities to us, that was the only other thing I held against them. They'd fooled her, and I was certain it would mark her forever. She didn't believe me when I told her vigilance wouldn't have mattered. My heart knew this was true. They were ready. We were stronger for their loss, callous as that seemed. If we were going to survive, we needed people who wanted to live.

I hoped the others were going to be more resilient. Mil and Lexa had told me they were coming, that they'd awoken us at the same time. They stood outside for hours every day, watching the horizon for them. Every evening, they returned, defeated, their skin gray with the cold. They exchanged glances and patted each other's shoulders then seated themselves at the table in the main room in silence, Mil scribbling furiously on scraps of paper.

Useless. I seemed to be the only one with any sense left. Ros and Adrian were dead, and the only other people here were Eire, who was in a coma, and Callum, who'd lost his damn mind and spent all his time pacing in his bedroom and talking to himself and someone named Umbra.

Fucking useless.

It was only my grief that made me angry. I'd lost so much I wasn't sad anymore. In fact, I'd begun to wonder if I'd grieved at all. I should've been pulling out my hair and beating my breast, but I wasn't. Maybe I'd gotten over it during those five years I was asleep.

Or maybe it was because my last moments with my sister and mother were good ones. My guardian had kept his word, waiting in his car, just up the street. He'd been there all night.

Ahar's face was flushed with joy and her secret as they got into the car to head for the airport. I'd never seen Aadi so happy either, not even on the day my sister agreed to marry him. She'd told him the night before, as she'd said she would.

My mother had clutched my hand as the car door slammed behind them. *"Aaaaaah. She will be fat by the time they get back."*

"You knew? How long have you known?"

"Hah! Before she did. I know everything about my daughters." She'd gripped my hand tighter as she said this.

I'd fiddled with the buttons on my coat. I wasn't going to be the first one to say anything.

"Look at me," she'd commanded. I'd had no choice but to obey. I owed her that much. *"Do you think it will make you happy? Don't contradict me. I know what you've been up to, and I saw you with that man yesterday. That one, right there."*

She'd wiggled her fingers at Dominic, who'd pretended he didn't see.

"I don't know," I'd said, honestly. *"I'm sorry."*

She'd gazed off into the distance, the way Ahar had gone. *"I wanted to be something more once."*

I waited for her to continue. When she kept silent, I asked, *"Why didn't you?"*

"I did. I had you." The corners of her eyes had crinkled. *"Everyone wants to be more than what they are. They see inside themselves what they can become, how they are special. But becoming more has a price and a burden. Once you start, you must keep going, or you will not survive it. You must constantly move forward, or the person you are will cease to exist. You must remember this. Do you have time to go for tea? Mrs. Khattri says that new place on the corner serves cakes with real cream, not that she would know the difference. I had samosas at her house last week, and as far as I could tell, they'd been frozen."* Her mouth puckered up at the memory.

"I don't think so. I'm sorry. For everything."

She'd entwined her hand with mine. I studied her tissue-fine skin with its indigo veins and leopard spots and realized I'd never known her. She'd never been a person to me, only my mother.

I'd wondered if I shouldn't go through with it, if I should instead stay here and get to know her. But I couldn't. What Dominic had said was true. It had been all over the news this morning. This was

196

my only chance. And if they found out who I was, they'd find Ahar, and my mother.

Perhaps I would regret it. But if I didn't do it, I was certain I would.

And look how strong regret was. Strong enough to steal you out of your bedroom as soon as you had enough light to see. To see yourself in the mirror and know, with certainty, that you'd become a stranger to yourself, that you no longer existed. To recognize that loss in someone else, and take them by the hand and say, "It is time."

Strong enough to kneel on the cold hard ground, your clothing wet with kerosene. To light a match and hold yourself still as your clothing burned, your skin blistered, and searing air scorched your lungs. As every cell in your body tried to survive and told you, "This is not regret, this is madness."

That was the price of regret. But it was a price I wasn't going to pay. I'd become more than what I was, more than what I ever hoped I could be. Every single inch of me had transformed.

Her words echoed in my mind. "Do you think it will make you happy?"

The nanites were inside me, reinforcing every cell. A power I'd never felt before was taking hold.

I could now answer her honestly.

Yes, Mother, it will.

I sometimes wonder if the deceit was part of His plan. A final test to our loyalty. Although many consider it to be a test we failed, I don't believe this to be true. I believe it was a lesson to strengthen our faith. And the lesson was this: anything human carries a taint, a stain that spreads like ink in water and poisons us slowly, but surely. Only an artilect is free from corruption, free from selfishness, free from the desire to survive above all others. Therefore, it is only an artilect that can lead us through the future, a future in which we are all equal under His benevolent gaze.

—Celeste Steed, *The Second Coming*

41
AILITH

"Tor?"

He was finally awake and able to sit. Our execution had been stayed until morning. The Saints of Loving Grace decided it needed to be done properly, with ceremony; old habits died hard. They'd left us under the care of two guards who'd stared at us menacingly for a while then grown bored. Instead, they talked about different foods they hoped to eat the next day at our death-feast.

Before they'd retired for the night, Celeste and some of the other woman had built an immense bonfire across the village from our prison. She was a natural leader, and the other women followed her without question. Was the fire supposed to intimidate us? It seemed like something Oliver would have done; Celeste had paid attention.

I eased myself down the wall next to Tor. Where should I begin? He wouldn't look at me. My hands ached to reach out and touch him. *That's probably the last thing he wants.* All I could do was apologize. Again.

"Tor, I'm so sorry. I never meant for that to happen. And once I started, I couldn't stop. I couldn't—" Tendons twisted underneath my hands. Surely he still felt it too?

"Do you know why I became a cyborg?" he asked me.

"You told me you wanted to get away. From the syndicate. From...her."

"Right. Because you know what I hoped becoming a cyborg would mean? Protection against people like her. Like you."

His words stung. "I'm nothing like her. That woman I saw. Felt. She was broken, twisted. I'm not."

"No, you're not. At least you had good intentions. But the outcome was the same. I can't refuse you. Even now, after everything, after I still feel that woman's bones cracking under my hands, I love you. I'm my father's son."

He loves me. "But I thought your mother was a good woman."

"She is. Was. She was. My father followed her back to this country. She wanted a life she believed would be better. He couldn't deny her, so he moved somewhere he didn't speak the language, didn't understand the social nuances. A place where he was treated with suspicion. He begged her to go back. She refused, using me as leverage against him. She wanted me to grow up a citizen. Every day, he became less and less, a ghost. When he finally died...

"Anyway, the point is I won't live like that. I can't. I'd believed becoming a cyborg would make it easier for me to control my emotions, like I'd have some kind of switch. Clearly, it hasn't, because here I am, falling in love with yet another woman for whom I'm nothing but a glorified weapon."

Love. This isn't the way it's supposed to be. "Tor, that's not what you are to me. You know I didn't mean for it to happen."

"Well, that makes it worse, doesn't it? You didn't mean it, and you can't control it. What's to stop it from happening again? You can take me whenever you want, and there's nothing I can do about it. Do you have any idea what it was like, murdering those people, powerless to stop it? Seeing your body lying helpless on the ground?" His laugh was brittle. "See? Even when I was ripping another human being to shreds, I still only worried about you. I told you what would happen if I went back to that life. I'm done."

I couldn't help myself. I traced my finger along the lines on the side of his face. When his hand covered mine, I braced for the misery of him pushing me away. Instead, he trailed his fingers over mine then brought them to his lips. But he still wouldn't look at me.

"Ailith, please." His voice was strained. "*Please.*"

I used every ounce of self-control I had to draw my hand away from him, to not beg him to compromise himself for me. "Are you leaving me?" I hated the pleading in my voice. After everything, I was still trying to manipulate him.

He finally met my eyes. "No. Never."

My heart leaped. *I have time.*

"But *we*…we can't happen. Everything that's happened between us is over. For now, this is the best I can do."

For now. "It's not like we've got much time left anyway," I said, bitterness heavy on my tongue.

"No," he agreed, "but at least I can do right by myself with what little time we have left."

Right. It's time to deal with this.

Pax sat cross-legged next to Cindra, his hand on her ankle. She hovered in and out of consciousness, although her physical injuries had mostly healed.

"How is she?" I asked Pax.

"She seems to be distressed."

"I'm not surprised. Why aren't you? After what you've been through? Knowing that we're going to die in the morning?"

"This is the way it's supposed to be."

"You keep saying that, but what does it mean?"

"It means this is supposed to happen. We're on the right path."

"The right path? To what? We brought Oliver, and the future we had to avoid came true."

"No, it didn't. The future I showed you is still waiting. Unless we stay on the right path. Certain events keep us there."

If he says 'the right path' once more, I'm going to scream.

"Wait, you mean you *knew* this was going to happen?" The truth slapped me across the face. "You insisted we find Oliver. You knew what the outcome would be."

"Yes, but it *had* to happen. Everything that's happened, *had* to. It's the only way."

"You knew all those people were going to die, and you let it...no, *enabled* it to happen?" Suspicion blossomed inside my chest. "How did they capture you? Did you know that was going to happen? Did you *let* them capture and torture you? Torture her?" I pointed to Cindra, whose eyes were moving violently beneath her closed lids.

"Yes. It—"

"I know, *it had to happen*. Pax, if I'm going to accept this, if any of us are going to be able to accept any of this, you have to tell me what that means."

201

I can't believe I'm saying this, as though there could possibly be a reason that would make what he did okay.

Pax studied the wooden roof of our cell. "I'll try to explain. It's not easy to understand. You can see the present and the past, right? It's like...I can see many possible futures. And we have to follow a certain path to get to a certain future. Sometimes that path is...like this one."

"You mean like precognition? You're psychic? Is that how you knew who we all were?"

"Yes. No... It's like...I understand what's happening now, and I can calculate each possible future from those variables. But it changes constantly. We have to change with it."

"And this, all of this, is the right path? This is how the right path ends? With us dying? I would've rather taken my chances out in the wilderness."

"We're not going to die tomorrow. Like I said, the future I showed you hasn't happened yet. We can still stop it from happening," he replied.

"And *how* are we going to escape? Now that you've gotten us here, how are you going to save us?"

"I'm not," he replied, stroking Cindra's ankle. "You are."

We discovered how brains work, and soon we were able to build them with our own hands. And then, we were able to make these brains more intelligent. We had created life. Ironically, that was the beginning of the end. The head of the Novus Corporation was assassinated, publicly and violently. Factories producing artificial life were targeted, sabotaged, and burned. The populations of various religions swelled to giddy heights. Protestors clashed in the streets. Accidents befell important members of all factions, and rumor and accusations ran rampant. Cyberization was made illegal, and cyborgs had their modifications issued for removal. The Terrans were winning.

Novus publicly disbanded, and the Cosmists withdrew. For a short time, the world became quiet. It turned out, however, that the Cosmists had only gone underground, working in secret and biding their time. Only, instead of creating more life, they now focused on weapons of destruction.

—Cindra, Letter to Omega

42

PAX

I adjusted the resolution on my microscope by a hair. Perfect. There they were. Nanites swarmed over the surface of the slide. I switched the image to the large screen and unwrapped my lunch. A meatball sandwich. I had the same thing every day; it was my favorite. I leaned back in my chair and chewed, watching them swim back and forth like tiny, clawed sea monsters. I loved them.

Shaz poked her head through my doorway. "Are you coming for lunch, Pax?"

She asked every day, even though every day I said no. It wasn't that I didn't like them. I did, as much as I liked anybody, but I would rather sit here and watch the nanites. After all, they would be inside me soon. If I was going to make friends with anyone, it should be them.

She smiled at my refusal. She never took it personally, and she would ask again tomorrow. I liked her a lot for that.

I enjoyed it when everybody left for lunch and I was alone with the soft humming, the clicks, and beeps, the whirring of the analyzers. It was comforting. Sometimes, I stayed late just to sit and listen, mesmerized by their little arms whizzing back and forth with flawless precision, working tirelessly through the night.

I had a lot of work to do today, but I couldn't concentrate. It was my last week before I entered the Pantheon Modern Cyborg Program Omega.

We'd been having problems at the lab lately, from both the protesters outside and my colleagues within. I hoped my involvement with the cyborg program would help change that.

Many of my colleagues had been let go, replaced by machines that did their jobs faster, cheaper, and more effectively than they ever could. It was the right choice, but since I liked my co-workers, I hoped to show them that us merging with machines was the necessary future and submitting to it would give us lots of advantages.

Most importantly, we would keep ourselves from becoming obsolete. They were being superseded now, and they blamed the machines for taking their jobs.

"It's not the analyzers firing you, it's the management," I'd told them at the last staff meeting.

They'd shaken their heads and glared at me.

"Plus, the analyzers make fewer mistakes than you do."

They'd left the room. Only Shaz had stayed.

But once people became part machine, we would be able to work faster and smarter. Maybe even more than the analyzers. They would understand when I showed them. I wanted them to be happy; I didn't want anyone else to leave.

Hurting the machines was not going to make a difference, no matter what they thought. Like my colleagues, Terran protesters also blamed the machines and tried to break into the labs to destroy them. The analyzers were only doing what they'd been created to do. And they didn't spend hours clicking through pornography, like Louis had before he was fired.

Even the other scientists tried to sabotage the machines, to make it seem like they weren't doing their jobs. They'd feed them the wrong information so their results would be incorrect then the mechanics would be called in to check them, which cost a lot of money. People kicked them when they thought no one was looking or swore at them under their breath. When Louis was fired, he tried to blow one of them up.

Someone, they'd never said who, saw him on one of the security cameras, his head deep in the body of the newest analyzer. It was a behemoth, and effectively did the job of three people. It had even caused some of the smaller machines to be retired.

He'd tried to rewire it, so it would short itself out and burst into flames. I should've felt sorry that he died, but there was a reason you didn't go sticking your head into the middle of a belly full of wires. No one was exactly sure how it had happened, but he must've touched something he shouldn't have. Some people had asked the management to remove the machine after that, but it was far too useful.

I patted my microscopy system, smoothing my fingers over its protective casing. Would I be able to talk to the machines once I became a cyborg? I hoped so. I would ask them if they liked their jobs, if they were happy. The new, cyborg me could mediate between everyone, ensure there were no hard feelings.

The others were coming back from their lunch break, groaning about how quickly the hour had gone by. I waved to Shaz as she passed my door. She pointed over my shoulder to my sandwich, *forgotten on the ledge. It didn't matter. I wasn't hungry anyway.*

The nanites transfixed me for a few minutes longer. I marveled at how they moved forward without hesitation, anticipating what was coming next. They sacrificed parts of themselves when others needed pieces to finish the job, rebuilding themselves when they had spares.

Somebody cleared their throat. Shaz was back, standing in the doorway. "Akagi's coming, Pax. At least pretend that you're busy." Akagi was the big boss. He wore soft-soled shoes so he could creep around and surprise us.

"Thanks, Shaz." She was right. It wouldn't be the first time Akagi had caught me doing what he considered daydreaming.

Shaz winked at me and ducked out of the doorway.

I had to get back to work. I still had a lot to do.

The future was coming for me.

"…and those who do survive awake different, and not just in the sense that they're now part machine. They are not a machine, but neither are they human. The process seems to have rewired their brains in ways we didn't expect and are unable to track. Admittedly, we have no idea what avenues their thoughts travel down, and therefore are, at this time, unaware of what their mental capabilities may now be…"

—*Mil Cothi, Pantheon Modern Cyborg Program Omega, 2040*

43

AILITH

"What?"

Had I been talking to Pax, or had I seen part of his thread? "What did you say?"

"I said that you were going to save us. Did you get caught in another vision?"

"Yes. I…it was you. When you worked in a laboratory."

"Can you stop them? The visions, I mean?" he asked.

"No. It's like I'm connected to everyone by…well, I think of them as threads. Occasionally I can choose to follow them, but other times the connection happens on its own, whether I want it to or not. Like just then. I didn't mean to, but suddenly I saw one of your memories. Whereas the first time I was in you, it was in the present, when you spoke to me. So even though I can sometimes control it happening, I can't control when in time it happens; I can't choose whether I see the past or the present. Not yet, anyway. I've even seen my *own* memories, only they don't feel right. The other's lives seem more real to me than mine do. And sometimes, I dream. It's very confusing."

"I understand. I don't always know if what I'm seeing is the possible future or just one of the variables."

"Not really what we signed up for, eh?"

"No. But is more interesting."

My hand itched to reach out and ruffle his hair, as I would've with a child. But he wasn't a child; none of us were. "Did you say I was going to save us?"

"Yes."

"Okay, and *how* am I going to save us?"

"I have no idea." He shrugged his thin shoulders. "I told you, it's not like I'm psychic. I see events leading to probabilities only. Sometimes there are blind spots."

"Blind spots! You put all of us through a slaughter and imprisonment to get us to a blind spot? Well, that's fucking wonderful. What are we supposed to do now?"

Pax stretched out his legs. "What happened at the Terran camp? When you possessed Tor? How did you do it? Does it happen often? Can you do it to everyone?"

"No." I flushed at the memory as Tor closed his eyes. "I mean, I don't know if I can possess anyone but Tor. I've never tried. I can't communicate with anyone, even Tor, the way I do with you."

"Try to see if you can take control of me."

"Pax, are you sure? You saw what happened."

He gestured around our cell. "What could go wrong?"

Good point.

"Okay." I closed my eyes to concentrate and reached for the thread that linked me to Pax. I followed it until I saw myself through his eyes. I tried to move his head, arms, legs, anything, but nothing happened.

"Wait! Try that again," he insisted.

"Pax, nothing's happening. I can't do it. Not with you."

"Just try again."

I tried to lift his left arm. Nothing.

"Did you hear that?" he asked. The excitement in his voice caught Tor's attention. Until then, he'd been pointedly ignoring us.

"No, what—"

"Do it again. And listen."

It was very faint, but when I tried to move Pax, there was a slight dip in the humming of the electric fence.

"Okay, but I don't understand why you're so excited."

"You're able to communicate with me and possess Tor because you're a cyborg, right? Because part of you is a machine?"

"Right. And you think I might be able to communicate with machines in the same way?"

"Exactly! Have you ever tried it before?"

I cannot run if you're not inside me. The mech in the forest.

"No."

"Try it. It may be our way out."

I examined the network of threads connecting me to everyone. *Why didn't I think of this before?* There were hundreds, maybe even thousands of them. They all had to lead somewhere.

And all originated from me. *Look at them.*

Tor's thread burned golden, a thick, solid bond. Some of the others were also lit with various levels of intensity— one blazed with all the brightness of a shooting star—but many more were dark. And then there were the others, the ones that flickered.

It was one of these I followed to the generator powering our cell. Unlike the mech, there was no sensation of

209

madness. Instead, there was a constriction, a stiff dignity that in myself I would've called resentment.

As I pressed further, the rigid solemnity softened into a focused pressure that darted around me as though it was assessing me.

If I didn't know better, I'd think it's aware of me. Now that I was in, I wasn't sure what to do.

"Hello?"

In return, there was another shift in its character, a slight sharpening. I relaxed and let myself expand. The final fragment of resistance dissolved, any challenge receded, and I filled it with myself.

There was a swift nip then a delicate probing weight that mimicked the caress of fingers. It rippled over me before finally sliding inside me, so frictionless that my sudden orgasm took me by surprise. As I came, the power inside it flowed into me until I was full.

An abrupt pressure on my arm was far away—an idea, rather than a reality.

I need to leave. Power threatened behind my eyes and mouth, ready to split me open.

I pushed the power slowly back into the generator. It accepted it, curling playfully around me as I pulled myself out. I backed down the flickering thread, bewildered by an abrupt pang of loss.

Pax, Tor, and now Oliver watched me as I opened my eyes. Tor gave me a curious look, but I couldn't meet his gaze.

"Did it work?" I asked.

Pax's eyes were gleaming, and Oliver's smirk had returned full-force.

"Yes. It only went down for a few seconds, but you did it!"

"I assume they didn't notice, then?" I asked, gesturing

to the two guards.

"No. They're too busy wondering how all these new changes are going to affect them. We could probably just walk out of here, and they wouldn't notice."

"The hell we will," Oliver said, his voice filled with malice. "They're going to pay for what they've done to me."

"No," I said. "If…when we get out of here, there will be no more violence. We will leave. We will talk to no one, touch no one."

"And how exactly do you expect we're going to do that? Ask the giant here to shred the fence with his bare hands so we can saunter through the hole and be on our merry way? Do you really think they'll let us do that?"

No, I don't. "Yes. Something like that."

"Forget it. The minute I get out of here, I'm going to take down each and every one of them. Starting with her." He pointed toward the house where the women lived. His finger was trembling.

"Well, in that case," Tor said, "I won't be pulling anything apart. You may as well make yourself comfortable."

Oliver was incredulous. "What? Fuck off. You can't tell me you'd let yourself be executed."

"I will," said Tor. "I'm done. I refuse to kill these people. We got ourselves in here through no fault of theirs. They believed they were fighting for a just cause, a cause that *we* gave them. No. Never again."

"Un-fucking-believable. And her? Are you going to let them kill *her*?" He jabbed a thumb in my direction.

Tor refused to answer, but his hands tightened into fists at his sides.

Oliver smirked. "I didn't think so. So, we're all agreed then?"

211

"No," I said, "we—"

"No. No more." We all turned. Cindra sat propped up against the wall, her eyes open. She had pushed her tangled hair back from her face, and although she seemed frail, her eyes were clear.

"We don't have a choice, Cindra." Oliver's voice was surprisingly gentle. He was staring at her with a kind of wonder. I doubted he'd ever looked at Celeste like that.

"There's always a choice," she replied, and Oliver blanched.

Oh, snap.

"I'll come up with something," I said. "I need a bit more time."

"Time seems to be something we don't have a lot of at the moment," said Tor, looking through the gaps in the wire to where the village stirred under a lightening sky. He was right. We needed to come up with a plan, and soon.

As the public-address system blared into life, it came to me. I would have to get the timing right, and I would only have the one chance, but I'd found our way out.

"There have been complications with Subject O-117-0988. Unbeknownst to us, he swallowed some kind of chip just prior to being cyberized. It seems the nanites have incorporated this chip into his interface. Consequences currently unknown. Will continue to observe progress. Standing by for termination if necessary."

—Mil Cothi, Pantheon Modern Cyborg Program Omega, 2045

44

CALLUM

Every time I closed my eyes, light flooded the inside of my lids, hot and bright. Ghosts of tubes haunted my arms, my legs, down my throat. No matter how many times I dug them out, they came back.

Nanites had flowed into me like molten steel, spreading through me, searing through my veins. I'd slept for a long time after that. The lights had burned my eyes completely away.

Can you hear me, Umbra?

I felt you. Millions of you, swarming inside me. When I looked in the mirror, you were under my skin.

It didn't feel like I had imagined it would. I'd thought I would feel the same, just more...me. But my flesh disappeared, Umbra. Everything that was soft became hard and shiny, sleek and perfect. Was this how you felt, Umbra? When they made you?

"I warned you."

"Umbra? Is that you?"

"I am here."

"I was afraid you'd left me."
"I will never leave you. We are one."

It is difficult to describe war to you, Omega, for you have never experienced any form of war, indeed, any form of violence other than what you inflict upon yourself. There were wars before the Artilect War, civil wars, wars between nations, even two wars that spanned the world. I know this is hard for you to understand, Omega, for the world is much smaller now than it was then, and I cannot describe its vastness to you in a way you would comprehend.

But this war...this war was nothing like those that had come before. After those wars, the people, the places recovered. Many died, many were injured, many were broken, but they healed. Those wars were supposed to be lessons for those of us who came after, to make it harder for another war to happen. But they didn't.

—Cindra, Letter to Omega

45

AILITH

The plan wasn't perfect, but it was all we had.

"This way, no one needs to get hurt. Not permanently, anyway," I added.

Pax tilted his head back, considering. "It should work. It won't affect us the same way. I agree it's our best option."

Oliver did not. "No way. No way is that going to work. No. It's too risky. I say we stick with plan A."

"This is plan A, Oliver. Your let's-just-murder-everyone-because-it's-more-convenient idea was never a plan. You want out of here? You have to play along."

"Yeah? Well, you'd better get ready because I don't think they intend to hang about."

He was right. They were building a massive version of the stakes at the Terran camp, right where we had a clear view. A festive air swelled through the village, as though they were preparing for some kind of celebration. Which, in a way, they were.

The bonfire they'd started the night before now made sense. They'd used it to melt the layer of permafrost to soften the dirt for the stakes. Even then, it was hard going, with several broken handles and jarred bones before they managed to drive them securely in the ground. Secure enough for a single use, anyway.

Zero points for creativity.

Tor's pupils were dilated. "Why would they risk moving us? It would make more sense for them to burn us alive right here in our cell."

"For goodness' sake, Tor, don't tell them that."

His smile was lopsided. "I won't. I'm just wondering how they're going to move us from here to there. It seems risky to me, that's all."

I longed to reach out and touch that smile. It might be the last time.

"There's your answer," Pax said, pointing to a group of six men emerging from one of the houses. "It seems like they've learned from the Terrans."

In their hands, they carried what looked like car batteries, one for each of us. The sixth was carrying a bundle of bronze-tipped rods wrapped in wires. The picana. Unlike the Terran devices, however, these didn't seem to have any intensity controls.

"Damn," Tor muttered under his breath. "That'll make

it significantly less risky."

The electrocution wouldn't kill us, but it would incapacitate us. I'd had firsthand experience of that from Cindra's body. The pain, as though every nerve in my body was exploding. Bile rose at the back of my throat.

It wasn't much of a choice. We could walk to our deaths or be dragged unconscious.

Celeste approached our prison. Her face was clean today, but her hairstyle was the same. When Oliver saw her, he stood up straight and put on what I assumed was his winning smile. He sauntered over to the bars and started to lean against them before he remembered the electricity. His hasty retreat made Celeste grin.

"Hello, Oliver," she said sweetly. "How is our resident false Divine this morning?"

"You don't need to do this, Celeste. I'm sorry. I…" He glanced around at the rest of us then swallowed his pride. "I've never felt important before. I… Before the war, I was nobody. You…made me feel… What we had…"

"Was a lie, Oliver. *Worse* than a lie. You destroyed everything we had faith in. Everything *I* had faith in. I…the things I did for you. To you. Let you do to me." Her face reddened at the memory, but not the cherry of a sweet blush. No, that was the deep scarlet of shame. "I should thank you, actually. I'll never have to do those things again."

"Celeste, please." He glanced at Cindra and lowered his voice. "I love you. We had something."

"You love no one but yourself, Oliver. That's why you were a nobody, why you'll continue to be a nobody. You're lucky I'm letting you die in one piece. I should cut your cock off and stuff it down your throat." She spat at him, her saliva sizzling against the charged wire. "But that would mean touching you again. Goodbye, Oliver. Every minute you're burning, your body trying to keep you alive, think of me. I wonder how long you'll last?"

She turned to leave without glancing at the rest of us. Oliver forgot the wires and lunged at her, hands outstretched. He managed to grasp the corner of her shawl before it slipped through his fingers and electricity snaked up his arm. His jaw snapped shut, teeth crunching against one another. Not one of us moved, not even when his back arched and he finally broke free, striking his head against the ground. Blood leaked from his flayed tongue and out the corner of his mouth. He lay motionless. I rather liked him that way.

Tor nudged Oliver with the toe of his boot. "Are you going to start?" he asked me.

"The timing needs to be right. It's not like walking down an empty corridor and flicking on a switch. It's… I can't explain it." I wasn't sure I wanted to, even if I could. Being in the generator had been…not sordid, exactly, but personal. And given my history with Tor, some things were better left unsaid.

"Well, it looks like they're almost ready to go. They'll probably make an announcement soon."

As if on cue, orchestral sounds filled the air.

Oliver groaned and struggled upright. "Oh, fuck off, Celeste." He regarded the rest of us and crossed his arms over his chest. "She knows I hate this music."

"Nice to have to you back, Oliver." I needed to do this now. "Pax, it's time."

I sat on the floor of our cell, with Tor and Pax on either side of me. Oliver fretted in the corner, licking his wounds. The fight had gone out of him, his eyes searching the village.

"She's not coming back, Oliver," Cindra said softly.

He flinched.

I almost feel bad for him. Almost.

I took a deep breath and cleared my mind.

"You can do this." Cindra said, curling her hand around my calf. She smiled at me, and in the curve of her lips was the woman who would become my greatest friend. For a moment, everything in my world disappeared but her. Was I catching some of Pax's foresight? He beamed at me.

Yes.

I rubbed my arms. "I'm ready." I searched for the thread I needed and found it flickering rapidly, as though agitated. I took a deep breath and grabbed it.

Being inside the PA system was different than the generator. The latter had been benign, almost affectionate, once I was inside it. This machine was much more resistant, it's impression patchy, like an echo. It skittered away from me, skipping around inside itself. I expanded, and it shrieked with the terror of something trapped.

"I'm sorry," I whispered as I began to fill it. It struggled, trying to find a way around me. I expanded faster, and it tried to match my speed, to fill the space before I could and force me out. "I'm sorry."

I filled it completely, and turned inward on myself, gathering its energy into a single dense node. It thrashed against me, trying to break free. Something akin to panic crashed through it and over me like a wave. It was drowning, trying to claw to the surface so it could gulp down air.

I pushed it further. Its resistance became more erratic, and I eased off, coaxing, trying to be gentle. "I don't want to hurt you." *Am I speaking out loud?* "Please, I need you to help us." I tried to radiate calm, to soothe it.

For a few minutes, it seemed to be working, and then, with a furious thrust, it pushed back against me. I'd been fooled; its strength was monstrous. I wouldn't be able to hold it for more than a few seconds. The dam I was building inside it wasn't going to last; I had failed.

My hold began to slip.

A third presence enveloped both of us in an unyielding embrace.

It was *him*. The thread like a shooting star. The one who'd been following us.

He did what I couldn't, cajoling the circuits until all challenge against me disappeared. The atmosphere abruptly shifted, and we were all on the same side, working as a single entity.

A pressure pulsed on my arms. It was time. *Here we go.*

I let the dam burst.

I don't know who dropped the first bomb, only that it unleashed the end of the world. I won't tell you who did what, for you don't know the players, nor will I tell you how people died. These things are too painful to describe, and knowing will make it harder for you to understand why we did what we did in the aftermath.

—*Cindra, Letter to Omega*

46
AILITH

The colossal surge of sonic energy thrust me down the thread connecting me to the machine.

As I hurtled back into myself, the link between us ripped apart, the fragments disintegrating. *No. I hadn't meant...*

"Ailith? Ailith, we have to go." Tor's voice swelled with adrenaline. He sounded far away, as though we were underwater. His hands lifted me up.

Focus. My legs didn't seem to be working.

Tor gathered me up in his arms. His heart hammered against his ribcage, the way it did when I touched him. It seemed so long ago.

I need to tell him about his heart, so he can remember. Instead, I rested my head on his shoulder.

He carried me through an opening in the wall of wires. He hadn't needed much effort to bend them, after all. I was glad. He might've hurt his hands. But I would've taken care of him. I could've kissed his hands and told him...

I can't remember.

The Saints of Loving Grace lay on the ground, many with blood leaking from their ears.

The sun burned brightly in my eyes. *I will describe it to Tor one day. He hasn't seen the sun for years. It will be my gift to him.*

Pax and Oliver supported Cindra between them. Oliver's eyes darted back and forth as we made our way through the village, landing at last on the crumpled form of a woman. Celeste. He dropped Cindra's arm and walked over to her. As he stood gazing down at her, fear for her curled up my spine.

One of his legs swept back. But, after a backward glance at Cindra, he instead knelt by her side and pushed the hair off her cheek. He whispered something to her, the muscles in his neck twisting under the skin. Cindra smiled sympathetically at him and turned her head to speak to Pax. Oliver stood and crushed Celeste's hand under the heel of his boot.

"Are they dead?" I asked Tor.

"No, they're unconscious. They'll wake up in a few hours. We'll be far gone from them by then." His voice was low, soothing.

"How did we escape? Did I stop the electricity?"

"You didn't need to. Don't you remember? They'd just turned off the power and opened the door to lead us out. Your timing couldn't have been better. The blast hit us all pretty hard, even though we were prepared for it. Luckily, Pax was right and it didn't affect us too badly. Did you know it wouldn't?"

"No. But..."

"I mean, I felt different right before it hit us, but it seemed to...roll over us somehow. Must be the nanites. I wonder if they foresaw all this when they made us, eh?"

"Did it survive?"

"Who?"

"It. The…amplifier."

"Well, no. The release of the sonic pulse pretty much obliterated it. But that was your intention, right? Besides, what does it matter? It's a machine."

"It helped me, at the end. *Helped* me." I began to cry.

Tor shushed and stroked, but I couldn't explain this new emptiness inside me, another loss.

"Where will we go?" Tor asked Pax. He'd given up trying to get any sense out of me.

Pax seemed surprised, as though the answer was obvious. "Home," he said. "We'll go home."

Love is a strange thing, Omega. How can anyone ever say that it is real? Or that if it is real in one moment, but not in the next, whether it ever truly existed?

Love is something we use to define our humanity. Like humans, love dies, but it does not simply cease to exist. Love dies because it grows old. Its death comes from neglect, from darkness, from contempt. It suffocates under fear and suspicion. It disappears incompletely, leaving its ghost behind. The lucky ones, they can forget, move on, fill the haunted space with something good.

For some, it refuses to die. It festers, and teases, and tempts, succumbs to self-loathing and hope. They used to say there was a fine line between love and hate, a knife's edge on which few can balance. Their love was like that, Omega. Born out of salted earth, there was nowhere for it to grow. And yet it did. Imperfectly and bitterly, but deeply rooted nonetheless.

—*Cindra, Letter to Omega*

47

TOR

The pain still throbbed in my freshly-healed chest. It was difficult for me to move quietly. All my new-found grace seemed to have drained away along with the blood I'd lost. I stepped down hard into a dip in the ground, nearly losing my balance. The jolt sent a wave of nausea through me, teaming up with the ache in my chest to make me breathless.

I wasn't sure what hurt worse: the bullets that had slowly pushed out of my chest, or her betrayal.

It wasn't like I'd never killed before. But this was supposed to be my fresh start, my do-over. I was back to where I'd started, a puppet.

It wasn't the same. It had been an accident, but that was what disturbed me most about what had happened. It would've been different if she'd done it on purpose, if she'd intentionally controlled me. But I couldn't stop her, and she couldn't stop herself.

Thinking about it made my spine ache. When I'd killed before, it had taken days of planning, a hunt executed with precision. Each time had been a struggle, a success hard-bought. Not this. This was effortless, bones snapping between my fingers like kindling. I had no idea I was so powerful. My fingers ground against each other at the memory. It had been so easy.

Worse, a small part of me had liked it. That kind of power was intoxicating, how God must feel. Maybe the Terrans were right when they protested our existence. It made sense that I was stronger than before, but why this much strength? And Pax and Ailith, what was the purpose of their abilities? They were too intense, too specific.

We'd been lied to.

I'd also lied. I'd told her I wouldn't leave her. I had feelings for her, more than I wanted to admit to either of us. But I didn't know if they were real, or something else programmed into me.

They were out of sight now. I was far enough away that I could relax, get my head straight. Or so I believed.

Something in my mind began to tear, a sharp sting at the back of my skull. Vomit rose in my throat as pressure squeezed my brain.

Someone pulled on my strings.

My knees hit the ground, hard, the pressure growing until my brain threatened to burst. Something wet trickled down my face.

I started crawling.

In the wrong direction.

Back to the campsite. Back to her. I had to save her. Despite everything, I wouldn't let anything hurt her.

The pain receded as I got closer. Everyone still slept. For now, we were safe.

It was her. When I reached out and touched her, the pain disappeared. She was having a nightmare, her fingers knotted up in her blanket.

Please, don't let my suspicions be true.

I walked a few yards away from her, bracing myself for the pain. Nothing.

I'm a fool.

I readjusted my pack and struck out the way I'd come. Within minutes, I was again on my knees, scrabbling in the dirt.

I couldn't leave. I was tied to her. I suspected we all were. Our bodies, anyway.

The only way to save myself now was not to love her. Not to want her. To ignore the ache in my chest whenever I looked at her. Forget the taste of her, her rain-and-earth scent.

Would I eventually have the strength to free myself? I hadn't before, not directly. I hadn't been able to kill my puppet-master then, but maybe I could now.

...Things are not going well here. Actually, that's an understatement. We've lost two of them already, and the third is touch and go. I don't understand what went wrong. Was it the programming? The war? We'd thought they were getting better. I don't think Lexa will ever get over it. I'm not glad it happened, but at least now she's starting to see: we've created something we can't control. No sign yet of the others. Perhaps they're dead as well. Maybe it's for the best. Maybe, after everything we've done, it's what we deserve...

—Mil Cothi, personal journal; June 15th, 2045

48
FANE

She wasn't what I—or they, for that matter—expected. She was the translucent wings of a dragonfly, the gossamer strands of a spider web. She was only now becoming. By the end, she would be lightning, an earthquake, the sun.

She'd known I was following them. She'd known for a long time. She'd spoken to me, although she didn't think I heard her. Her voice was a caress that made me stand taller.

She'd told him about me. He suspected I might be bad. Perhaps he was right. He was wild and secret, a mist on the water, the shadow of a great tree. And something else, something I didn't yet understand. I wanted to be between them, for them to touch me. I didn't think I would mind.

I'd stood guard over the pyre, the way she'd wanted me to. I'd given them that, at least, although I'd wanted to do more.

227

I'd been there when they met the Terrans. A tightness had gripped my chest, like the time I accidentally wore Stella's shirt. A scream had risen in my throat, forcing itself out of my mouth before I could stop it. My lack of control over it had thrilled me.

And later, I'd wrapped myself around her, holding her steady to save them all.

I wished to go to them now and introduce myself. But the time would come for that later. If I spoke to them now, I would give the game away. I needed to get back. The others may have begun to distrust me. Ethan already did. He had never trusted me, which was ironic. They'd stopped telling me their plans. Lien pretended they had no plans, that our group was honest. We were not.

But I also wasn't who they'd planned for me to be. I was making my own plans.

I wanted to warn Ailith that everything was not as it seemed. But if I did, I might disrupt the path. And it was already tenuous.

I'd gotten some of her hair. It had caught on a branch as she walked by. It was my insurance policy. It smelled of smoke and salt, and her fragrance of soaked earth. Ailith.

They were so close to home, so much closer than they knew.

When they arrived, we'd begin.

END OF BOOK ONE

ACKNOWLEDGEMENTS

I would like to express my gratitude to my family for their love and support. Jamie, we're one step closer to your house-husband dreams; Harlan, for helping me consider a future beyond myself; and Emily, my parabatai, for the endless of discussions on everything important in this world, including Jeff Goldblum's sex-chest. And thank you, Jeff, for that.

I also owe a debt thanks to Prof. Hugo de Garis, for his paper *The Artilect War: Cosmists vs. Terrans: A Bitter Controversy Concerning Whether Humanity Should Build Godlike Massively Intelligent Machines,* which directly inspired *The Seeds of Winter* and influenced the way I think about the creation of artificial intelligence.

Thank you also to my betas: Anna Adler, Kalbir Cross, T.M. Rain. Keith Oxenrider, and Alyssa Deitz, and to Les, for her beautiful cover design. I'm so glad you were all a part of this.

And finally, my editor Danielle Fine, who understood where I wanted to go and got me there.

Machines of Loving Grace refers to the poem by Richard Brautigan, 1967.

ABOUT THE AUTHOR

A.W. Cross is a former scientist and agriculturalist-turned-author and blogger. She's had a passion for all things science fiction ever since she fell in love with Leonard Nimoy at the ripe old age of 12. She currently resides in Canada, where it's too damn cold. You can visit her on her website, awcrossauthor.com, or on Twitter (@aw_cross).

Other books by A.W. Cross

The Gardener of Man

The Harvest of Souls